LUSTS OF THE FORBIDDEN

Lusts of the Forbidden

Valentina Cilescu

Delta

Copyright © 1999 Valentina Cilescu

The right of Valentina Cilescu to be identified as the Author
of the Work has been asserted by her in accordance with
the Copyright, Designs and Patents Act 1988.

First published in Great Britain in 1999 by
HEADLINE BOOK PUBLISHING
A HEADLINE DELTA paperback

10 9 8 7 6 5 4 3 2 1

ISBN 0 7472 4829 X

Typeset by CBS, Martlesham Heath, Ipswich, Suffolk
Printed and bound in Great Britain by
Mackays of Chatham plc, Chatham, Kent

HEADLINE BOOK PUBLISHING
A division of the Hodder Headline Group
338 Euston Road, London NW1 3BH
www.headline.co.uk
www.hodderheadline.com

Lusts of the Forbidden

Prologue

Clive scratched his crotch reflectively. '*How* many?'

'Like I said. Three pairs, right up her front. Bloody spectacular I call it.'

'You're having me on.'

Fat Roland threw his colleague the A4 envelope. 'Take a look at the photos if you don't believe me. Heh, heh, you could have a bit of fun with them, know what I mean?' The photographer tossed half a doughnut into his open mouth. 'A man could die happy.'

Clive slid the photos out of the envelope and whistled. 'Blimey. Here, Greg, take a butchers at the melons on this. Good, eh?'

Greg Usher glanced over Clive's shoulder on his way back from the coffee machine. Sure, the model was a bit of all right – if you liked a girl who could wear three bikini tops at the same time – but frankly he'd seen it all before. When you worked on a rag like *Mondo Bizarro* you could only stand to see just so many freaks before you started fantasizing about vicarage tea-parties and elastic support-hose.

'Stuck on,' he commented as he flopped down in his chair. 'You can see the join.'

Clive sniffed. 'You're only jealous 'cause I'm doing the interview.'

'Just remember what I said when they come off in your hand. Now, where's that flaming article ... ?' Greg sorted through the teetering pile on his desk. Oddly-shaped vegetables, mutant lobsters in the Channel Tunnel, alien invasions of Milton Keynes – they were all there. Oh, there it was: *They walk among us – aliens in the West Midlands.* Greg stifled a yawn.

'What's eating you, big boy?'

He looked up to find his editor perched on the desk beside him, tall and voluptuous in a soft grey business suit that made the most of her endless legs.

'Nothing.'

'Not been missing out on our beauty sleep, have we?'

Greg grunted. 'I'm fine.'

'So you've finished that feature on sexual magic then?'

'I'm . . . er . . . still working on it.'

Cindy folded her arms, pushing her small, quivering bosoms closer together. 'Still? Be honest, Greg, you haven't started it yet.'

'Yes I . . .'

'Don't bullshit me. Listen, I can't keep putting it back to next month's issue. The punters want Tantric sex and plenty of it.'

'There's a lot of research to do,' Greg protested. It was true, too; there was a lot of research, he just hadn't been doing any of it and Cindy knew darn well he hadn't.

She leaned over him, filling his nostrils with the scent of her perfumed cleavage. 'Well, you'd better get on and do it then, hadn't you?' Her index finger wagged teasingly in his face. 'Or I might have to keep you in after school again.'

Cindy went off to populate Fat Roland's wet dreams, leaving Greg staring after her. He was bored. Bloody bored. It was a crime to admit it, but he was even bored with Cindy's backside, and that was tantamount to saying you were dead from the waist down.

That backside was just about as perfect as a

backside could get. It was round and smooth, and as downy and firm as a giant white-fleshed peach: the kind of arse that lent itself effortlessly to tight basques and a good hard spanking. He ought to have been delirious with lust at the prospect of another late-night session over the photocopier – but he wasn't. Frankly, he'd only let her seduce him because he thought it might relieve the boredom – well, that and the faint hope that if he shagged her senseless, she might be so grateful she'd have him transferred to somewhere marginally more exciting, like *Carpet Tile Quarterly*.

Chrissakes, he was a sports reporter! He wasn't cut out to rot as second string on a third-rate monthly. If it hadn't been for that incident at Hurlingham with the girls' polo team, he'd probably still be with the old crowd at the *Daily Comet*, blagging Cup Final tickets and spending Friday afternoons down the pub with Andreas Hunt.

Hunt. The name jolted him back to the present, and the other article he was researching: a series about alien abductions. Not that he believed for one moment that Andreas Hunt had been kidnapped by little green men. Knowing Hunt, he was currently holed up on the Costa del Crime with the contents of the petty cash and a lifetime's supply of lager.

All the same, there was no denying the run of weird disappearances over the past few years. TV presenters, business tycoons, all sorts; even the odd politician, not that they were any great loss to society. Some had disappeared for a few days or weeks, only to reappear with a sudden taste for religion, or right-wing politics, or red PVC. One or two had vanished without trace. Like Andreas.

It was a complete mystery: one minute on his way to Whitby to interview the local MP, the next . . . gone. Oh, there were rumours, of course. Persistent ones. And it was hard to avoid them on *Mondo Bizarro*. When your readership boasted an average age of seventeen and the combined IQ of an ant, there were always rumours. The current favourite was vampirism. God, people could be so unoriginal. One guy had even suggested that Hunt had been bitten by a vampire and resurfaced as Leader of Her Majesty's Opposition. OK, so there was a faint facial resemblance between Andreas Hunt and Anthony LeMaitre . . . but then again, some people reckoned Fat Roland looked like Claire Rayner.

Usher checked his emails, fidgeted around a bit and gazed out of the window. It was raining again. He thought of the long, soggy walk he was going to have to the Tube, just to talk to some loony who thought Anthea Turner was a werewolf.

Life was dull, dull, dull. 'Why doesn't anything interesting ever happen?' he lamented, out loud.

'Watch what you wish for, mate,' counselled Sy, the smart-alec MSc who read Stephen Hawking for fun. 'It might come true.'

And sure enough, it did.

1

From the audio diary of Andreas Hunt

Two things. First, I am not Andreas Hunt. Well OK I am, but I don't look like me and this isn't my body. Oh, shit, that doesn't make sense; where's the rewind button?

Start again. I *am* Andreas Hunt. Got that? Hack journalist on the *Daily Comet*, the man who brought you 'Man Eats Own Foot' and 'Prince Charles Marries Rubber Plant'. That's me. Or it used to be.

Anyhow, second thing. Having to pretend to be a sex vampire isn't all it's cracked up to be. I'm living in fear that one day he's going to find out – the Master – and then me and Mara . . . well, best not to think about what he might do to us. But it's weird the way life turns out. One minute you're penning lurid little exposés for the *Comet*; the next,

7

some vampire vixen's ripping your clothes off and this bloke who reckons he's an undead sorcerer is trying to nick your body.

God, I hope there's plenty of tape in this machine. It's going to be a long, long story.

Laverton on the water, Gloucestershire, 1 June

Sylvie Montana shuddered with renewed pleasure as her lover's tongue flicked wetly over the hard pink crests of her nipples.

'*Non, non*!' she gasped. 'No more, I can't . . .'

Christian laughed and rolled her onto her back, forcing her legs apart with his thigh. 'I want you again, Sylvie. And it's no good pretending, I know you want me too.'

He was right, of course. The very first time he had touched her, he had seemed to know every trick to turn her on. She let out a low, soft moan as his thigh rubbed against the dripping wet mound of her pubis, already soaked with their mingled juices. 'It's too much, Christian, too much!'

He bent low over her and nuzzled into the nape of her neck, nibbling at the soft, warm skin. 'There's no such thing as too much, didn't anyone ever tell you? Just lie back and let me do this to you . . .'

Forgetting her resolve to be strong with him, Sylvie abandoned her pleasure to Christian's expert hands. He slithered down her body like a snake, his strong arms possessing her, his teeth nipping playfully at the skin of her breasts and belly as he drew a long, moist trail to the heart of her sex. It was sheer, unadulterated torment, and she adored it. When his tongue burrowed deep into the tropical heat of her cunt, parting the dark pink folds that crinkled around the secret bud of her clitoris, she threw back her head and howled like all the hounds of hell were after her.

Things had moved bewilderingly quickly since she arrived in England. A couple of weeks ago, she had been at home in France. Until she received the solicitor's letter, she had almost forgotten about Mireille, her grandmother's eccentric cousin, who had scandalised the family by running away at sixteen, to live with an Englishman. And she was stunned to learn that the old lady had died, leaving everything to her.

Not that 'everything' amounted to a fortune. All the same, it wasn't every day that someone died and left you an English antique shop. Sylvie wondered if she ought to feel guilty, seeing as she'd never even met her grandmother's cousin; but it was impossible not to be excited by this unexpected windfall.

She got out a map of England, and found the Cotswolds. She'd never been there before, but everybody said it was lovely, very English; well, if nothing else, it would be an adventure. And Sylvie could use an adventure or two in her life: working in a Paris dress shop was not the most exciting of jobs, even if it did sell *haute couture*.

A few days later, she was there. Laverton-on-the Water was everything she had imagined it would be: with its butter-yellow stone cottages, winding streets and sparkling river dotted with moorhens, it had the kind of chocolate-box charm that drew the tourists in on photogenic summer Sundays. Unfortunately, you couldn't say the same for Tante Mireille's antique shop.

Once upon a time, the sign over the door might have read 'Quality Antiques', but the paint was so blistered and faded it was almost impossible to tell. The shop occupied the front room of a decrepit cottage, tucked away behind a derelict shed at the ugly end of the high street. The moment she pushed open the door and walked into the overpowering stink of mildewed wood, Sylvie's heart sank. This wasn't an antique shop, it was a heap of old junk that nobody in their right mind would ever want.

She stood in horrified silence, staring at the jumble of unwanted clutter: the rusted mangle, the upturned chair with its seat hanging off in rotting canvas shreds, the bulging cardboard boxes of mouldering books. And her eyes filled with tears of disappointment.

'Hi,' said a voice behind her. She swung round, hastily wiping her cheek.

'I'm afraid the shop is not open today, monsieur. My aunt . . .'

The dark eyes crinkled at the corners. He was young, he was handsome, he smelt of fresh, clean sweat. 'It's OK, I just wanted to say hello.' He stuck out a hand, and his grip was as firm as she had hoped it would be. 'Christian Saunders. I own the house opposite.'

'Sylvie Montana.'

His fingers caressed hers for a long moment before he let go. 'Looks like you've got a lot on your plate here.'

She sighed. 'Yes. I hardly know where to start.'

He smiled. 'Well, if you could use some help sorting through it . . .'

That night he cooked dinner for her. She knew
he was watching her intently as she ate, his eyes
devouring her full, plump breasts through the
diaphanous white shirt she'd worn just for him. It
made her feel excitingly sluttish to feel his eyes
follow the quiver and sway of her breasts as she
leaned over to fill his wine glass; and she loved
that feeling. She had never felt more desirable in
her whole life.

'You're beautiful,' he commented, as though he
was remarking on the weather.

She looked up at him through long, dark lashes.
'No, I'm not.' Her tongue curled round a sliver of
honeydew melon. 'My legs are too short and my
bottom is too large.'

He laughed. 'I've never heard such rubbish in
all my life.' He intercepted her fork as it travelled
towards her mouth again, took the piece of melon
into his own mouth and kissed her, pushing the
sticky sweetness between her lips. 'You're the
sexiest woman I ever met.'

She licked the juice from her lips. Could he see
that she was trembling? 'Do you say that to all your
women?'

'Why should I care about other women? The only
one I want is you.' Christian reached over and

unfastened a button on her skirt. 'I want to fuck you, Sylvie Montana.'

Fuck. The earthy Englishness of the word sent shivers running through her. She was no blushing virgin, she knew she had a great body; and she'd had men before, plenty of men. But this guy, with his almost arrogant confidence and the dark sensuality in his eyes, excited her in ways she was almost ashamed to admit.

They were in the bedroom doorway when he stopped to kiss her and began to strip off her blouse, easing the zipper down with a long, slow 'zizz'. She murmured with pleasure as his hands pushed up her skirt, baring her stocking-tops, and began kneading the soft springy cheeks of her backside.

'Oh yes. Oh yes, that feels so good.'

He chuckled softly. 'And this will feel even better.'

She felt his fingers slide beneath the lacy edges of her white silk panties, and let out a gasp as his fingernails teased the tight brown mouth of her anus. 'Not there . . .'

'Don't tell me you've never let a man touch you here before? Relax, just let yourself go.'

Her tiny whimper of protest melted into pleasure as his fingertip breached her last virginity, plunging into the tight, hot heart of her backside in a sudden stab of possession. A flood of hot wetness soaked her panties as he slid down her body and began to kiss her pubis through the white silk, all the time finger-fucking her in the arse, with such skill that her legs trembled and she had to clutch at the doorframe to stop herself falling.

His mouth was white-hot on her flesh, his breath coming in burning waves that made her swollen clitoris throb with delicious anticipation. And when he tore down her panties and began to tongue her sex, it was more than she could take.

'Please,' she gasped, as the terrible warmth took over her whole body. 'Please fuck me. Please . . . make me come.'

'Not yet.'

Her hands clutched at his dark curls, forcing his face against her pubic bone. 'I can't bear it!'

But he paid no heed to her protests. His tongue flicked again and again over the hypersensitive bud, sending flood after flood of sex-juice trickling down her thighs. She was so close it seemed impossible that she could hold back any longer, but he was skilful; he knew how to take her to the very brink and hold her there for what seemed like an eternity.

Her orgasm came suddenly, clenching her pussy

muscles and making her scream with the intensity of it. Before the last waves of pleasure had died away, he was carrying her towards the big brass bed.

She could not have resisted him even if she had wanted to. One moment he had her clit in his mouth, the next she was lying face-down on the feather mattress, skirt up round her waist and her buttocks bare, save for her white lace suspenders.

Sylvie felt his dick before she had even seen it. It was huge, so thick and hard she was sure it would split her in two as its fat, bulbous tip thrust between her arse cheeks. Suddenly afraid, she cried out and tried to wriggle free, but he plunged into her in one swift sword-thrust that left her helpless and gasping with savage pleasure.

Her hands clutched convulsively at the crisp white sheets as he rode her like no man had ever ridden her before; her backside bucking up to meet the hot, hard slap of his balls against her moist buttocks. It was not love; it was not even romance.

But hell, it was fun.

The man in the grey overcoat had just had the kind of day you tried to push to the back of your mind. Delayed flights, cancelled meetings, and to make matters worse his wife had faxed him an ultimatum about Holly. Why couldn't women be civilised about these things? Men needed sex like they needed to eat; and would you want to eat nothing but baked beans, day after day, for the rest of your life?

He sat in the airport departure lounge, drinking Carlsberg and staring morosely at the TV screen. Bloody *Neighbours*. She'd be watching it, too; he could picture her squatting on the sofa with her box of All Gold, waiting for him to get home so she could give him another ear-bashing. And all because he screwed the occasional secretary. What man wouldn't screw a girl like Holly, given half a chance? 42-26-36, brainless and gagging for it – let's face it, she had the lot.

'What gate for Dublin, mate?' asked a man with a small child in tow.

'Dunno, they haven't announced it yet. But it's usually 61.'

'Oh. Right.' He sat down and hauled the child onto his lap. 'No, you can't go for a wee-wee, you've only just been.'

The man in the grey suit glanced back at the screen just as the words 'News Flash' flashed up, followed by a picture of Ten, Downing Street. He cocked half an ear; you never could tell when something might happen to affect the price of pre-stressed concrete.

'. . . was announced an hour ago that the Prime Minister, Mr Harry Baptiste, was found dead . . .'

'Good God,' exclaimed a middle-aged woman. 'Turn it up.'

'. . . police are investigating, but at this stage they are unable to confirm that . . .'

'*Dead?*' blinked the young father. 'Harry Baptiste? In a *massage parlour?* I don't believe it.'

Neither did anybody else. Baptiste's government might have suffered from a few sex-scandals over the last couple of years, but Baptiste himself was so clean he was practically antiseptic. A murmur of astonishment ran round the assembled travellers.

'Flight JR668 to Dublin, boarding now at Gate . . .'

Nobody was listening. They were too busy crowding round the television screen.

'. . . and Baptiste's deputy, Lawrence Manifold, will be sworn in as Prime Minister later tonight . . .'

'Don't know why you're all so surprised about Baptiste,' sniffed a woman with the kind of lipsticked mouth that looked like a bad razor slash. 'He was a man, wasn't he? If you ask me, all men

17

are the same – dirty-minded animals, you can't trust them further than you can throw them.'

'Oh, for fuck's sake!' snapped the man in the grey suit, pushing past her on his way to Gate 61. Good on you, Harry Baptiste, he thought gloomily as he trudged towards his reluctant reunion with Sandra. At least you died with a smile on your face.

Sylvie stood naked in Christian's kitchen, watching him make penne al'arrabiata.

'I thought English men couldn't cook.'

'Then you don't know much about English men.'

She perched on the corner of the table, flicking her dark hair over her shoulder. 'I don't know anything about you.'

He laughed. 'What's there to know?'

'Oh, I don't know really . . . where you come from I suppose, what you do . . . That would be a start.' Sylvie glanced around the expensively nouveau-rustic kitchen, all copper saucepans and solid oak cupboards. 'You must have a very good job, to afford a weekend cottage like this.'

He took the pasta off the heat, turned round and cupped her breasts in his hands, pinching her nipples between finger and thumb. 'None of that matters. This is all that matters.'

She growled, half in protest, half in pleasure. 'Don't, Christian – I want to know! Why won't you tell me?'

He chuckled, flicking his tongue lightly over the engorged stalk of her right nipple. 'I'm an interior decorator, I do up rich people's houses in London and they pay me obscene amounts of money. Satisfied?'

Sylvie sensed that she would have to be. This time he bit down on the fleshy stalk, and her knees buckled under her. On the hob, the arrabiata sauce was boiling away to nothing, but she couldn't have cared less. There was a different kind of hunger in her belly.

'Christian . . .'

'You want me, Sylvie. Don't tell me you don't.'

She kissed and licked the salty flesh of his torso, and felt his hardness as he slipped between her thighs. Reaching out, she unfastened the top button of his trousers, slid down his zipper and the smooth, hot rod of his dick sprang into her hand. Its tip was as smooth and slippery as wet glass, its constant ooze of clear fluid fragrant and sticky on her fingers. She ached to have it inside her.

'Fuck me.'

'Not yet.' He flexed his hips, slowly drawing his

dick back and forth in the tight sheath of her fingers; and she felt it grow thicker, stiffer, the thick blue veins pulsing under the pink flesh. 'First I have a proposition for you.'

'A . . . ? What do you mean?'

He smiled at her puzzled expression, the slightly sullen pout of her lips. 'The shop. You need money, right?'

She frowned. It was so very hard to concentrate with his fingers pinching her nipples and his dick sliding rhythmically in and out of her fingers. 'You want to buy the shop?'

'Not the shop, just the stock.'

She almost laughed in his face. 'But . . . but there is nothing in the shop but rubbish, you told me so yourself! Why would you . . . ?'

He shrugged. 'Perhaps I'm just a nice guy.' He lapped at the trail of sweat dripping down the valley between her breasts. 'I'll give you a good price.'

Sylvie gazed up into his dark, fathomless eyes. She was no psychologist, but she could sense that there was more to it than that. There was something he wasn't telling her. 'I don't understand.'

'You don't have to understand. Just trust me.'

Trust. The word jarred. She lusted after him, sure she did; but trust? Her eyes drifted down from his face to his smooth, muscular torso, to his taut belly and the thick pink dick that called to her to take it deep inside her and think about nothing but fucking, fucking, fucking.

'You can suck it if you like, Sylvie.' Christian stroked her hair back from her face, and she shivered with unwilling need. His voice was soothing, coaxing, irresistible. 'Go on, take it into your mouth.' His right hand slipped between her thighs and began frigging her with merciless precision.

'Why say no, Sylvie? When it's so much easier to say yes.'

2

Andreas Hunt clicked off the tape recorder, threw it down and turned to his lover. 'This is a waste of time, isn't it?'

'No, it's not.' Mara rolled onto her belly, her auburn hair swishing over one shoulder to reveal a full, pink-tipped breast, the nipple pierced by a ring of glittering white crystal. 'You've got to try. Who's going to stop the Master taking over the whole world if we don't?'

'Yes, yes, I know.' He sat down on the edge of the bed. 'But no one's going to believe any of it, are they? I mean – would you?'

She smiled. 'Of course I would.'

Andreas gave her nipple-ring a playful tweak. 'You're a white witch; you'd believe anything. *He's* a journalist . . .'

'*You're* a journalist, Andreas. And just think of

all the things you've had to believe over the last few years.'

He thought. Magical severed penises, vampires trapped in blocks of crystal, the Prince of Wales spontaneously combusting on daytime TV . . . Whatever else you could say about his life, it hadn't been boring. Not many ordinary blokes could say they'd been stabbed through the heart, trapped in suspended animation in a block of crystal, resurrected in a different body and were currently masquerading as a vampire MP. About the only things he hadn't encountered lately were space aliens, and he couldn't even be sure about that.

'And you really think this tape . . . ?'

'I don't know. All I know is, you have to try. Baptiste's dead, Andreas.'

'And it wasn't the Master who killed him. At least, that's what he claims . . .'

'The Master's been trying to kill Baptiste for months,' Mara pointed out. 'Why would he lie now? It doesn't make any sense.'

'If you ask me, nothing makes sense any more.' Andreas threw a rolled-up sock at the wastepaper bin. He missed, and it flew out of the open window.

Mara walked her fingers up his thigh. It felt very, very good. 'Just tell it like it is, Andreas. Tell the story of how we got to be in this mess. If he's as good a reporter as you say he is, he'll nose around, find the rest out for himself.'

'I didn't say he was good. Just desperate.'

Mara's fingers snaked round his body, unbuttoning his shirt and slipping inside. 'There's only one way to find out. Make the tape and send it.'

Her hand slid a little lower down his torso, and his dick sprang to attention, straining painfully against the inside of his pants. Hunt let out a whimper of protest. 'I'm supposed to be at the House of Commons by half-past.'

'Look,' whispered Mara. Pointing at the clock beside the bed, she snapped her fingers and the second-hand froze in mid-tick. 'Ever wished you could make time stand still?'

'What the—'

'Now look at your watch. See? That's stopped, too. It doesn't work for long, but long enough to have some fun.'

Andreas blinked. 'Where did you learn to do that?'

Mara laughed and drew him down onto the bed beside her. 'I've been practising. And there's something else I'd like to practise . . .'

She unzipped his trousers and the red, glistening fruit of his cock-tip sprang to meet the tip of her tongue. But she did not take it into her mouth. Giving it a playful lick, she slid down over Andreas's body like a smooth, white snake, until she lay astride him and his dick was nestling in the deep valley between her breasts.

He groaned and flopped back onto the rumpled bedcovers, his freshly pressed grey suit squashed instantly into a million creases. Not that he cared. It was hard to care about anything much when a beautiful, big-breasted white witch was squeezing her tits around your dick like a couple of warm, fragrant pillows.

'Where were we?' She started moving gently back and forth, up and down, fucking him with her breasts. *In heaven, that's where I am right now*, thought Andreas.

If only time could wind itself backwards, to the first time he and Mara had fucked on the beach at Whitby. Back then they'd never even heard of the Master, or Anthony LeMaitre, or the hundred other names he'd been known by over the past four thousand years. And as for vampires, well . . . vampires simply didn't exist. The last person he'd expected to run into was a white witch called Mara

Fleming. Funny how a chance meeting could change your life. Or was it chance?

That beach. Hell, what a memory. For a precious hour his entire world had consisted of cool sand, warm breasts, a hot cunt that sucked like a tight wet mouth . . .

If only the rest of his life could be that simple.

Christian was not happy.

He'd made Sylvie a bloody good offer for the contents of Aunt Mireille's shop, and what had the stupid little bitch done? She'd told him she 'needed more time to think about it'. And not half an hour before that she'd been telling him she was thinking of setting fire to the whole shopful of junk, since nobody would ever want to take it off her hands. It was frustrating, it was irritating, and more than that: it was completely baffling.

Not that he had any intention of taking 'maybe' for an answer. As far as he was concerned, 'maybe' meant 'yes', and the word 'no' simply didn't exist. Besides, he couldn't afford to let this slip through his fingers; there was too much at stake.

The following morning, he put a bottle of champagne to chill in the ice-box and went across the empty street to Sylvie's shop. A bee buzzed lazily around a clump of hollyhocks, sprouting out of the overgrown drains. A cat slunk lazily across the pavement and stretched itself out in a pool of warm sunlight. Christian smiled. The day was going to be hot and so was Sylvie. This would be easy; all he had to do was persuade her to come across to his house for breakfast. A little wine, carelessly spilt down the front of her clingy white blouse, a little caviar licked off her succulent, smooth-skinned body, and she would be begging him to take anything he wanted.

The blinds were up and the sign dangling on the inside of the door read 'Open', but when Christian reached out to turn the handle he found it would not budge. Strange – she never locked the door. He rattled the handle. Nothing. Shading his eyes, he peered through the slatted blind into the shaded interior of the shop.

His jaw fell open, and his dick uncoiled like a waking cobra. Sylvie was lying on her back on the shop counter, her mane of silky black hair hanging down and her red lips wide with groans of pleasure. Her white T-shirt and lace bra had been pushed up to reveal the twin fruits of her breasts, plump and lightly tanned, their stiffened stalks a dusky pink circled with coffee cream.

She was naked from the waist down except for a pair of high-heeled white sandals, her skirt and panties discarded on the dusty floor; and sweat glistened on her belly as she spread her thighs and arched her back to take another millimetre of her lover's swollen dick.

Christian's hand slid into his pocket, and he stroked his own erect prick as he watched the landlord of The Golden Fleece fucking Sylvie Montana's wet pussy. He was a big man in every sense of the word: six foot six, thigh-muscles bulging under his denims as his long, fat cock slid in and out of the tight wet tunnel between the French girl's thighs. It was slow, smooth fucking, but there was nothing passionless about it. Heat radiated out of Sylvie as she drew herself up until she was sitting with her thighs round the landlord's, and her fingernails clawing red ridges down his back.

Anger seethed in Christian, but it was more than matched by the hungry fascination that kept him staring through the glass into the shop. Watching the two figures coupling on the counter, the way Sylvie's red mount hung wetly open, a pearly trail of semen trickling from her lips.

She let out a groan of delight as the landlord slid out of her and hoisted her onto his shoulders, burying his face in the folds of her cunt. The groans turned to squeals of ecstasy as he tongued his own come from between her pussy-lips, thrusting into her with his tongue-tip, teasing her to another orgasm, and then another . . .

They must have stayed like that for almost half an hour, although Christian was so aroused that he had lost all track of time. All he could think of was how much he wanted to be the man between her thighs, how much he wanted to throw her over that shop-counter and show her that there could be no true pleasure without pain. But she was lost in a world of her own pleasure, far too absorbed even to notice him. Or so he thought.

Suddenly Sylvie slid down from the shop counter and walked across to the door. Her hair was dishevelled, her skin dripped with come. She had never looked more desirable in her life.

For a moment Christian thought she was going to unlock the door and invite him in. But as she reached the door she simply smiled, blew him a kiss, and turned the sign to 'Closed'.

Christian slammed the house door behind him.

'Bloody hell. Bloody *hell*.'

Storming into the kitchen, he marched straight

across to the corner cupboard and wrenched open the door.

'Out. Now!'

The petite, manacled woman who crouched inside gazed down at him with eyes as blue as a china doll's, bright with a kind of joyful terror. Beneath the white school skirt and tie, her tiny, braless nipples quivered with terrible apprehension.

'Please, sir, I . . .'

Infuriated by her failure to obey him instantly, Christian grabbed her by her two brown pigtails and dragged her out of the cupboard, dropping her onto the tiled floor like a sack of potatoes. She squirmed delightedly at his feet, the navy-blue pleated skirt riding up around her waist to reveal a bare bottom criss-crossed with fading stripes.

'Upstairs, schoolgirl!' he screamed, aiming a kick at her upturned backside. 'This minute!'

She ran away, and he heard the sound of her sensible black lace-ups thundering on the polished wooden stairs. Normally the anticipation of cruel pleasure would have relaxed the tension in his aching body, but all he could feel was a horrible sense of foreboding.

He went into the pantry and opened the tall, oak-fronted cupboard. Its contents were a peculiar mixture of the mundane and the perverse. Leather straps and paddles shared shelves with packets of dried pasta and spice-jars. Tins of tomato puree and anchovy paste were ranged alongside silver nipple-clamps, handcuffs and spiked collars.

Underneath the bottom shelf stood a line of canes and whips: everything from little pearl-handled riding crops to bullwhips and switches. Christian selected one of his favourites: a thick bamboo cane, which he oiled regularly to preserve its vicious suppleness. The fresh chilli juice which he was about to rub into it would give it that important extra bite.

But before he attended to his own recreation, there was something he had to do. He set the telephone to hands-free and made the phone call he had been dreading.

'Master?'

Anthony LeMaitre's voice came back, syrupy, threatening. 'Do not tell me you have failed.'

Christian swallowed. 'Not exactly, Master . . .'

The voice hardened. 'Tell me.'

'It seems the box's new owner has already been awakened, Master.'

'What!'

'And since we know she must give it up willingly,

or its power will be destroyed . . .'

'Fool!' hissed the Master, in a tone that sent cold shivers through Christian's corrupted soul. 'Imbecile! Can I not rely upon you to carry out even the simplest task?'

'Master, I—'

But the Master did not give him a chance to defend himself. 'Be quiet. I am sending the twins to do the job properly. And consider yourself lucky I am in a good mood today.'

The leader of His Majesty's Opposition switched off his mobile, and Christian was left cursing. He thought of the squirming little schoolgirl waiting for him upstairs, her bare backside offered up to the swish and cut of the cane. But even that thought did not bring him pleasure.

Damn. Damn and blast. He brought the cane down hard on the edge of the kitchen table. This was all he needed.

Alex Carlyle was a hustler; the kind of bloke who knew how to buy cheap and sell high. Strictly small-time, you understand, not the kind of scams where anyone got seriously burned – well, not yet, anyway. Because Alex was still waiting for his big break. Who could say, maybe it would come today.

He drove into Laverton-on-the-Water and parked his brand-new van in a side street. Best to go round the town on foot; today he was on the lookout for cheap Arts and Crafts furniture, and the last thing he wanted to look like was a dealer. He checked his hair in the rearview mirror, and gave himself a knowing wink. Young, nicely-spoken, floppy fringe . . . he could do that hapless Hugh Grant act to perfection, and it always knocked a few pounds off the price he had to pay to get what he wanted.

At first glance, Laverton wasn't as promising as he'd hoped. Too many cutesy little antique shops by far, too many people who knew exactly what things were worth. It wasn't until he reached the dingy end of the high street that he struck gold.

Funny, really. He'd been half-inclined to turn back, cut his losses and head for Cirencester; then he spotted the peeling wooden sign pointing to a tiny little shop round the corner: 'Quality Antiques'.

More out of curiosity than expectation, he followed the sign to the door of the most dilapidated antique shop he had ever set eyes on. Antiques? Junk, more like, to judge from the assortment of dented coal-scuttles and broken china arranged on the pavement outside. But as he reached the front door and peered inside, he realised that appearances could be amazingly deceptive.

'Good God.' He was dreaming, he must be. There was no other explanation for it. You just *didn't* turn a corner and walk straight into The Land that Time Forgot. He rubbed his eyes, but no, the dream didn't go away. The prices in the window were still twenty years out of date, and that gem of a William Morris desk was still sitting there, under a clutter of lampshades and tatty cardboard boxes.

A single thought raced round and round his head. He had to have that desk. No matter what he had to do to get it, he had to have it.

He raised his hand to open the door, then noticed the 'Closed' hanging sign. And no phone number to ring. Dammit. Well, he wasn't going to be put off by some stupid sign. He looked around for someone to ask, but there was no one. His mind digested the problem. OK, he'd knock. And if nobody came, well . . . he'd never actually done breaking and entering before, but there was a first time for everything. And if he left a few quid by the till, it wouldn't actually be stealing, would it?

He knocked. Nothing. He knocked louder, then

hammered. And at last something moved at the back of the shop. A girl. Quite young, a real looker too; shiny black hair, large breasts that had never seen a silicon implant, legs that went right up to her . . .

She walked towards the door, and he saw her sway slightly. Now he could see her close-to, he could tell that there was something not quite right about her. Something about her eyes . . . a vagueness. She was looking straight at him, smiling at him through the glass; yet he had the peculiar feeling that she was looking straight through him, not really seeing him at all. It was as if she was drugged. She wasn't wearing much either: just a damp T-shirt and a short black skirt that had ridden up, revealing one smooth, tanned thigh . . .

A chain rattled and the door swung open.

'Er . . . hello. My name's . . .' Alex never got the rest out because the girl grabbed him by the wrist and started dragging him across to the back of the shop.

'Take me,' she whispered, laying herself down on the desk like a sacrificial virgin on an altar. They were the only words she spoke.

Alex gaped. His lips went bone dry, his throat so tense he could hardly breathe. He looked down at the girl and she began to moan softly, pushing up her T-shirt and rubbing her breasts with the flat of her hands. Her thighs parted, and a sweet, heady scent of warm musk drifted up, enveloping Alex like a caress.

Without bothering to think about what he was doing, without even bothering to close the blinds, he bent down and started lapping at the skin of her inner thighs, pushing up her skirt as his tongue climbed towards the deliciously scented heart of her sex.

His fingers penetrated her, releasing a flood of juice that washed over them like the nectar from a crushed peach, sticky and sweet. It was probably dripping onto the polished surface of that priceless antique desk too, but what the hell? All he could think about was his sudden, insatiable sexual appetite. He didn't know who this woman was, he hadn't a clue why she was doing this; but he had to taste her, he had to have her, he had to fuck her.

The concentric folds of her inner cunt-lips swelled at the touch of his tongue-tip, and he felt a shudder of excitement tense her whole body, arching her back and raising her at least two inches from the surface of the oak desk.

It was more than he could bear when she started clawing at his shirt, pulling off the buttons, in her haste to get at his nakedness. He kicked off his shoes and wriggled out of his trousers. If someone had bothered to come to the front door of the shop and look in, they would have seen two semi-naked bodies writhing on the desktop; but even if giant earwigs from the fifth dimension had chosen that moment to land on Gloucestershire, it is doubtful if Alex Carlyle would have noticed.

The girl slid from his grasp and rolled onto her belly, getting up on her hands and knees and offering him her beautiful rump. He closed his eyes for a moment and let his hands slide over it, exploring every dimple, every tiny hair, delighting in the smooth coolness of the skin, the soft plumpness of the two tanned cheeks. And then the hunger overtook him, and as she pushed herself against his hands he speared her on his cock, letting out a long, shuddering groan as the glass-smooth pussy swallowed him up like a greedy mouth.

Even as he rode her, Alex could not quite believe that this was happening to him. Here he was, fucking the most sensationally hot babe on top of the antiques find of the year.

Waves of luxurious warmth crashed over him as he plunged his dick into her, right up to the hilt. It was incredible, like fucking on a tropical beach.

In fact, you could say it was the best fucking day of his life.

3

'We had sex on the beach . . . oh boy, it was good.
Amazing, like . . . like mind-sex. I know that sounds
stupid, but it's true. You ever had sex with somebody
and it feels like she's fucking your mind – no, your
whole soul – not just your body? No? Well I'm
telling you, it beats a quick fumble on the back row
at the multiplex . . .'

I'm rambling again, thought Andreas, clicking
off the dictaphone for a moment so he could clear
his head. It wasn't easy. Every time he thought about
Mara he got a hard-on, even sitting here on a
freezing cold toilet in the House of Commons. He
wouldn't have been skulking in here at all, but it
was the only safe place he could think of to record
the next instalment of his audio diary. One thing he
definitely couldn't risk was the Master getting his
hands on it and finding out that his devoted

parliamentary private secretary, Nick Weatherall MP, was in fact hack journalist Andreas Hunt. One false move, and he and Mara would be well and truly stuffed.

He made a fresh start. 'Anyhow, when I woke up, Mara was gone. But I couldn't get her out of my mind. I knew I had to find her. I asked around and got a few leads, and I stopped for a bite to eat at this service station and . . . well . . . there was this really horny girl hitchhiker, see.

'She said she was from Romania, an exchange student or something. Not that she was, of course; but I didn't find that out till later. To be honest, I don't remember a lot of what she said, 'cause I was trying to drive and look down the front of her top at the same time. She wasn't helping. I mean, could you keep your eyes on the road with a girl jiggling her tits in your face? They were huge, but kind of round and perky, and she wasn't wearing a bra. And her nipples . . . talk about chapel hat pegs.'

Andreas cleared his throat and adjusted the bulge in the front of his trousers, wishing Mara was here right now. This wasn't a very big cubicle but it was amazing what you could get up to, with a bit of imagination.

'Nipples. Ahem, yes. Right. So there we are,

speeding down this country lane, and I'm talking a load of bollocks because it's not every day a girl gets in your passenger seat and whips them out for you, and you don't look a gift horse in the . . . well you don't, do you? Next thing I know, she's unzipped my flies and she's sliding her hand in and pulling out my cock.

'So what do I do? Bloody nothing, that's what. I grip that steering wheel and pray I don't wake up – because this has just got to be a dream, right? Only now she's going down on me, and I'm telling you, it never felt that good in a dream, it has to be real. You know, the way the tongue and the lips are all silky-smooth, but the back teeth catch on your cock-tip when she takes you really deep inside? Only real girls do it that way. Dreams are too perfect to be any fun, 'cause in dreams you *know* she's not suddenly going to take it into her head to bite your dick off. God, does that sound pervy or what?

'Where was I? Oh yes, driving down the road. Yeah, so she's sucking my dick and I'm getting ready to spurt; and to be honest if I'd not been so far gone I'd have been scared shitless, because that road was like a rollercoaster and with those tall hedges you couldn't see what was coming towards you round the next bend.

'Which is when it bloody well happens. I spurt, and right at that very minute this massive Land Rover comes hurtling towards me out of nowhere. Naturally I wrench the wheel over, but it's too late. Head-on collision they said, when I woke up in the hospital. Lucky to be alive. "What about the girl?" I say. "Is she OK?" "What girl?" they say, and they look at me as if I've got piss-stained trousers and a bottle of meths. "There is no girl. You were alone in the car, don't you remember?"

'Oh, I remember, all bloody right. I remember that the second I came into her mouth she smiled at me, with my spunk dripping down her chin, and then she vanished. Into thin air. Shazam. And *that*, my friend, was when I knew something *spectacularly* weird was going on.'

He leaned back against the cistern and clicked off the dictaphone, breathing heavily, not sure he wanted to remember. After a couple of seconds' silence, a voice drifted through the partition from the next cubicle.

'Er . . . excuse me, old man.'

Andreas shot bolt upright. 'What?'

'Sorry to bother you.' The voice was deeply apologetic. 'Only do you think you could go on talking for a bit? I haven't quite come.'

* * *

That night, Sylvie felt most peculiar – sort of drained, as though a high fever had raged through her body and left her empty and numb.

Things had happened to her, she knew that. Strange things, unbelievable things. She sat in front of the TV screen, a freezing-cold tub of ice cream wedged between her thighs, and stared in dumb amazement at grainy, black and white footage from the antique shop's one primitive CCTV camera. That naked girl having sex on the shop counter – was that really her? And the one making out on top of that beaten-up old desk?

It was like watching someone else play your part in a porno movie about your life. The thought was weird, scary, yet disturbingly erotic; and despite her tiredness, she began to feel a familiar heat begin to radiate from the pleasure-centre between her thighs.

Her hand strayed under the hem of her short black skirt, lingering on the mossy mound at the base of her belly, still bare for she had not bothered to retrieve her soiled panties from the floor of the shop. She closed her eyes and breathed long and slow and deep. If she rubbed just here, ever so gently . . .

A sudden, dry wind rattled the room, breaking the spell. Her eyes shot open.

'Why don't you let me do that for you?' It was a man's voice, quiet, shocking, compelling.

Suddenly there was a dark, dangerous man at her side, his eyes glittering at her from the shadows. Sylvie gasped. 'Who . . . who are you? Where did you come from?'

He did not answer, but bent over and scooped a handful of ice cream from the tub. Sylvie cried out as his fingers slid down the front of her T-shirt and smoothed the freezing cream into her left breast. She opened her mouth to cry out, but the man's eyes were mesmerising and she found she could utter nothing but a soft whimper of need.

Another hand, more slender than the first, dug deep into the creamy mess and let it drip into Sylvie's bare lap.

'Let me help.'

The woman's voice came from the other side of Sylvie. She had the same compelling eyes, an even richer, more sensual, more deliciously terrifying voice. Tall and dark with fine features and glittering eyes, she was the man's perfect feminine reflection. Twins, thought Sylvie, the thought surfacing through the torment of cold, creamy caresses. They're twins, they have to be. Two faces of the same creature, two aspects of the same, malevolent pleasure . . .

They seemed to know each other's thoughts, to anticipate each other's moves before they made them. With unearthly coordination, they began to reawaken her body, surprising, delighting, tormenting.

And then the pain began.

She winced as she woke up, rolled onto her back and felt every muscle in her body cry out in protest. Sunlight was pouring in through the open blinds, bright and accusing as a knife-blade.

She rubbed her eyes and turned her face away.

Where was she? *Who* was she? And why was she lying sprawled on the floor of the antique shop, her body bruised and bitten, scratched and soiled? For a second everything was a haze of mixed-up pictures, too fragmented and way too bizarre to make any sense. Then they clicked into place, like pieces in a jigsaw puzzle, and suddenly she remembered every tiny detail with painful clarity.

She wished she didn't.

Slowly, uncomfortably, she eased herself to her feet, forcing herself to look at her reflection in a chipped mirror hanging askew on the wall. Her black hair hung in matted clumps, her skin was scratched and caked with blood and semen and who could tell what else. Red weals round her wrists recalled the ropes that had bound her to the banisters as the two strangers forced obedience from her body. Her nipples ached from the imprint of the sharp-jawed clamps, and her bruised lips were swollen with the memory of a night of violent pleasures.

Oh yes, she remembered it all now. The male twin had been angry with her, so very angry. And all because she couldn't find a box he wanted. Her clitoris swelled as she recalled how savagely he had thrown her across the chair and buggered her, his cock sheathed in spiked rubber that burned as it pleasured. He had promised her such degradation. And she had wanted it so, so much . . .

But as Sylvie begged him to give her what she craved, the woman had stopped him. She had seized Sylvie by the hair and jerked back her head, forcing her to look up into those glittering dark eyes.

'She does not deserve it.'

'Please . . . !'

The man smiled thinly and peeled off his black leather gloves. 'You are right, she has not earned it. Perhaps we should leave her to think about her foolish disobedience.'

'No!' whimpered Sylvie, her whole body on fire with need. 'You can't leave me like this, you can't!'

The woman pushed her roughly away as she clutched at the hem of her skirt. 'Do not touch me, slave!'

The man took Sylvie's chin in his hand, digging his nails into her flesh. 'We will be back.' The promise hung on the air, menacing and sweet. 'But only when you can show us the box.'

Sylvie had begged and pleaded, but it was no use. The door slammed in her face and she was left lying naked on the floor, her heart pounding and her body aching for its just punishment. In that moment, she had understood; she was trapped, a prisoner of her owm desires. And there would be no respite from this awful torment until she could produce what the twins had demanded.

It was the middle of the night, but the hunger would not let her go. Sylvie knew that somehow, anyhow, she had to find that box. A fuse had blown the lights, so she took one of Aunt Mireille's old oil lamps and went down the bare wooden stairs into the shop. It was like descending into a crypt, full of mustiness and decay. Shadows danced and leered from the corners as she stood the lamp on the windowsill and began to search.

Increasingly frantic, she dragged out drawers, prised open cupboards, overturned tables, picked up boxes and emptied their contents all over the floor. Glass smashed, wood splintered, but all Sylvie cared about was finding that box, whatever and wherever it might be.

It wasn't there. And eventually, through sheer exhaustion, she had fallen asleep.

Picking up a dusty chenille rug, Sylvie wrapped it round her bare shoulders. In daylight, the mess in the shop looked even worse than it had the night before. It would take her all day to put it right – and then again, what was the point? The box wasn't there, and right now the box was the only thing she cared about. Because without the box, her new masters would not return and give her what she craved.

As she walked towards the staircase at the back of the shop, her bare toes struck something hard. Glancing down, she saw an old book lying face-down on top of a pile of old theatrical costumes. Casually she turned it over with her foot and saw the two words handwritten in elaborate French script across the front cover: 'THE BOX'.

Alex was feeling like a complete bastard.

It was a unique experience for him: as a rule, nothing would have made him feel better than knowing he'd just conned somebody out of a small fortune. But this particular scam kept on nagging at him. Hell, this was a fine time to start developing a guilty conscience.

You really are a cunt, Alex, he told himself as he contemplated his prize. I mean, first you shag a drugged stranger senseless, then you leg it with the ten-thousand-quid desk you just shagged her on. This time, you've really excelled yourself.

Mind you, he thought, if I'm a cunt I'm a bloody rich one. *And* I got laid, heh, heh, heh. He opened the workshop door to let the daylight in, and took his first proper look at the desk. It was even better than he'd thought. The spunk stains would soon polish off, and apart from one or two small scratches here and there (which just added character) the whole thing was flawless. Ten thou? Make that twelve, no, fifteen – that pewter scrolling was fucking exquisite.

He slid a couple of the drawers in and out, and very nearly orgasmed at the sight of the perfect dovetail joints. Taking one of the drawers off its runners, he held it up to the light. Wow, get a load of that quality. There was a bloke in Hampshire who'd cut his right arm off for a chance to own a piece like this.

Just as he was about to slide the drawer back in, he remembered something he'd heard about these desks. Crouching down, he peered into the gap where the drawer should be and slid in an exploratory hand. Bingo! The secret drawer slid open on hidden springs, revealing . . .

A box. And not just any ordinary box, either. Alex gasped as he picked it up and felt the weight of gold in it. *Solid* gold. The totaliser in his brain went wild as the figures ticked right off the scale. In his hand sat a box, roughly four inches square, cast in solid twenty-four-carat gold and set with jewels and mirrors. Sapphires, rubies, diamonds . . . oh, my God, he thought, rubbing his eyes; they really are diamonds, none of your cheap cubic zirconia. And they are *huge*.

He stroked the priceless treasure as though it were a lover's breast. Oh, boy. He'd always told himself the antiques business was nothing like 'Lovejoy', and here was the solid-gold proof.

It was a hundred times better.

Sylvie lay on her bed, reading her Aunt Mireille's journal in horrified fascination. It was crazy, everything about it was too off-the-wall to be true, yet something made her keep turning the pages, desperate to know what came next.

'The box possesses great power,' she read. 'It will show you the secret desire of any you view through the glass, and make you irresistible to them. But beware. Beware the price your soul must pay.'

For a moment, Sylvie felt a chill pass over her skin, raising the hairs on the back of her neck. Then she laughed and let the journal fall onto the bed. Last night, in the darkness, she might have believed. But in the cold light of day . . .

Her Aunt Mireille must have been even madder than she thought.

With the utmost care, Alex opened the hinged lid of the box.

Perfect. Absolutely breathtaking; he just couldn't believe it. The box must be what, two hundred years old? Maybe even three. And the mirrored interior was completely flawless, without so much as the tiniest scratch.

But what was this? He picked up the tiny gold-rimmed thing, attached to the inside of the box by a long gold chain. It was a magnifying glass, but what on earth for? It gleamed with a strange brilliance as he held it up to examine it; obviously it was just a trick of the light, but it seemed as though the glass grew larger and acquired a halo of milky brightness.

Strange. He rubbed it on his glass cloth, then held it up again, at the precise moment that a tall, blonde woman in country tweeds stepped through the door of his workshop.

And at that very same moment, a brilliant white mist collected inside the mirrored box, swirled like water down a plughole, then dispersed to reveal a perfect picture of the woman. Only this time she was not wearing her sensible brogues and her hacking jacket; she was naked and bound with leather, chained to a post, licking come off the floor . . .

Alex began to wonder if somebody had slipped something into his pint down The Dog and Fox, especially when a little voice – the woman's voice – popped into his head.

The voice was low and smooth, almost matter-of-fact. 'It all began with my first boyfriend, you see . . .'

All at once he became aware that the woman was talking to him. With a supreme effort of will, he dragged himself back to the present moment and snapped the box shut. Only seconds could have passed, yet he felt curiously dislocated from time, as though he had just done a round trip of the galaxy and arrived back before he set out.

'Er . . . hi . . . sorry, I was miles away,' he smiled.

'That's quite all right, don't mention it.'

She smiled back at him, and he noted that she was quite a looker, in a formal kind of way. Not the way she'd looked in that picture in the box. Not naked and submissive and begging for humiliation. He tried to chase the image from his mind.

'Can I help you?'

'I hope so. My husband and I are moving into the area – we've bought the Hall, perhaps you know it?'

Alex knew it. Matter of fact, he'd handled a bit of knocked-off silver from the old place when the last butler decided to award himself an unofficial pay-rise – not that he was about to admit it to the new lady of the manor.

'Quite well, yes.' The woman's shapely hips were quite a distraction, even encased in that tweed pencil skirt. He couldn't help imagining her out of it and on her knees, and him riding her the way she rode out with the local hunt. 'So you're looking to furnish the place?'

She tucked a stray wisp of blonde hair behind her ear, flashing a dazzle of diamond earring. 'Just a few nice country pieces . . . something comfortable for the sitting room perhaps. I was wondering if you might have something suitable . . .'

All at once his mouth felt desperately dry. 'Leather's a very classic look,' he ventured, looking her straight in the eye. 'Perhaps a nice leather Chesterfield . . . ?'

He saw her tongue-tip flick over her lips. 'Leather?' Her voice trembled.

'Leather. Maybe I could show you some? This is quite a fine piece.'

'Leather . . .' This time the word came out as something between a whisper and a sigh, and he felt her shiver as she ran her hand over the arm of the settee. He unfastened her skirt and pulled it down over her backside, and she purred like a she-cat, kissing the belt as he slid it from the waistband of his trousers.

She growled with ecstasy as the belt hissed through the air and raised a long, pink welt on her upturned arse-cheeks. It was true, thought Alex, his cock pulsing with exultation. It was completely impossible, but everything he had seen in the mirrored box was true.

Life just got better and better.

4

Andreas followed in his Master's wake, frankly shit-scared to be less than two paces behind a being who inspired such fear.

The 'Technology in Business' exhibition was a great PR opportunity for Britain's next Prime Minister, the Rt Hon Anthony LeMaitre MP; a place to see and be seen, to do deals and press flesh. More than that, thought Andreas as they moved from stand to stand; it was a power game. Some were here because they were desperate – they'd do anything to sell their product, even if it meant selling their soul along with it. Which it might well do if you sold out to the Master. Others were players; habitual gamblers who loved the game; greedy opportunist on the lookout for the right product at the right price, with the right sweeteners.

And then there were the outsiders. People like

Andreas Hunt, who took no part in the proceedings but just watched from a distance, alternately fascinated and revolted by the lengths people would go to get what they wanted. Voyeurs, thought Andreas, felling like a peeping Tom watching somebody else have sex. Well, it was one way to get your kicks.

The dictaphone in his trouser pocket bumped against his thigh, reminding him that he hadn't had an opportunity to add to the diary today. The trouble was, you had to be Houdini to get away somewhere quiet, even for five minutes, and even then there was the constant possibility that the door would burst open and some vampire slut or other would demand to know what the hell you were doing. This is a game, too, mused Andreas; but Trivial Pursuit it ain't.

As he shouldered his way through the writhing mass of delegates and stall-holders, it struck Andreas how similar the exhibition was to one of the Master's infamous orgies. Same twisting, throbbing knots of bodies, give or take the odd genital piercing; same overheated atmosphere; same stench of hunger and power.

He should have been listening to the Master, but his mind drifted back to the first time he had set foot in Winterbourne Hall, the finest and most dangerous whorehouse in all of England. This would go on the tape, he decided; you couldn't understand the Master if you didn't understand how it all began.

It was all to do with Mara Fleming. Not that it was her fault; she was just as much a victim as he was. But the fact remained that if Andreas hadn't tumbled head over heels in lust with the busty white witch with the violet eyes, he wouldn't have followed her when she disappeared. And if he hadn't followed her, he'd never have tracked her to Winterbourne.

The Hall was a well-kept secret. It lay buried deep in the English countryside, screened from prying eyes by acres of ancient woodland and miles from the nearest village. Abandoned after the Second World War, the once-magnificent building had been left to decay – until a lame man called Delgado appeared from nowhere, bought it and set about transforming it into a house of dark and secret pleasure.

It was around that time that famous and powerful people started disappearing. The rich, the beautiful, the influential, the glitterati. Some turned up dead and bloodless, some reappeared weeks later with completely different personalities. Some just . . . disappeared. Andreas didn't know it at the time, of course – in fact he'd never heard of Winterbourne Hall – but Delgado, and the sluts who came to work in the great house, were all under the mind control of the Master. And if the Master was to regain his former power, he needed two things: blood and sex. Which was where Winterbourne Hall came in.

Andreas could still smell the dizzy sweetness from the incense burners that stood around the Great Hall at Winterbourne. That first orgy . . . he had never seen anything like it. He should have run away, got the fuck out of there while he still had the chance, but would *you* pass up the chance to watch half of *Who's Who* screwing the other half right in front of your eyes?

He remembered every last, lingering detail . . . Gavin de Lacy, drunk on aphrodisiac wine, naked on the floor, a girl straddling his face and forcing him to drink her juices, a youth between his thighs, sucking his dick and buggering him with a springy hazel wand. Harry Blomfield, his bare buttocks whipped red by the switch of birch twigs, screaming with ecstasy as the girl bit down hard on his balls. That gorgeous coffee-skinned barrister with the heavy breasts and the sleek hips, taking two dicks into her mouth at once and a third between her lovely buttocks . . . The procession of blonde virgins, clad in nothing but diaphanous veils that revealed the rings in their nipples and the fine gold chains by which their mistresses led them. Yeah, he remembered all right; well, it wasn't the kind of occasion you were ever likely to forget.

There was a square, sunken pool in the centre of the hall. White marble with a flight of steps leading down into it. Scented pink waters and rose petals floating on the surface. Two African princesses getting it on in the water, frigging each other with a cake of soap while the men and women lying around the pool looked on with bulging eyes and longed to pleasure their own aching bodies.

It was a vivid image even now: the two dark bodies moving together in the warm water, lithe as seals. Then Calypso lying down on the mosaic pavement that ran around the edge of the pool, forced to spread her legs wide while her sister Sappho lapped every droplet of rose-scented water from her body, writhing and twisting and gasping until at last the long, muscular tongue plunged deep into her tight hole and she let out a long, high scream that echoed around the pillared hall.

'Weatherall!' snapped the Master, and Andreas

spun round, painfully conscious of the bulge in the front of his trousers.

He swallowed hard and tried not to look too priapic. 'M-master?'

A look of contemptuous rage passed across LeMaitre's face, and for one horrible second Andreas thought he had seen through his disguise.

'You are not paying attention, Weatherall.'

'No, Master,' admitted Andreas. He had learned enough to know that denying it was pointless.

The Master's eyes narrowed. My eyes, thought Andreas with a shiver. Strewth, but it was weird, looking into your own stolen face.

'Did you feed, this morning?'

'Er . . . yes.'

It was true, he had snatched a couple of rounds of toast and marmalade, but Andreas knew that was not what the Master meant. Sex-vampires did not eat toast; they fed on sexual energy.

'Hmm. Perhaps the energies were insufficient. You shall feed again before nightfall.'

'Yes, Master.'

They continued on through the exhibition hall, Andreas doing his best to make polite conversation and wishing the Master could develop an interest in football.

'Had I better get Ibrahim to bring the car round?'

'Not yet. I wish to remain here a while longer.'

He glanced at his watch. 'What about the Commons committee meeting at half-past two?'

The Master sneered. 'I have other priorities.'

'Oh.' Andreas didn't dare ask what. 'And will Christian be joining us?' he enquired.

The blaze of anger flared again in the Master's eyes and he wheeled round, so suddenly that Andreas took a step back and knocked over a life-size cutout of Bill Gates.

The Master's hand shot out and seized Andreas by the throat. 'You will *not* speak that name in my presence!'

Unable to breathe, let alone speak, Hunt managed a painful shake of the head and the fingers sprang open. The Master smoothed an imaginary speck of dust off his sleeve, turned on his heel and extended a hand to a passing businessman.

'Sir George, how wonderful to meet you.' LeMaitre's smile was dangerously compelling. 'I really must thank you again for your very generous donation to Party funds . . .'

Sir George beamed and basked in self-importance. 'Happy to contribute to the country's bright future . . .' He gave LeMaitre a hearty slap on the back. 'All for clean government, old chap. Keep up the good work.'

The Master watched him retreat with distaste. 'Imbecile.'

'Rich imbecile,' pointed out Andreas.

But the Master had already turned his attention to other matters. A slow, lascivious smile spread across his face as they approached a small, out-of-the-way university stand, advertising customised business courses.

'Ah,' he murmured. 'Dolores de la Fuerte Aranuez . . .'

Andreas blinked. 'Sorry? I got an unclassified in French.'

The Master sighed tetchily. 'Dolores de la Fuerte daCosta Aranuez, delicious Professor Dolores. A Brazilian, you know. Can't you tell from the sway of those hips?'

Hunt had to agree that she was something special. Exotic too. Skin the colour of lightly-toasted almonds, dusky lips slick with clear lip-gloss, shiny black hair cut into an unstructured bob that framed a face at once super-intelligent and innocently sensual. She was dressed in a close-fitting green jacket with a V-shaped neckline that offered tantalising glimpses of her breasts; and a short white skirt through which Andreas could just make out the faint outline of cream-coloured panties.

You could tell she wasn't used to dressing to kill; from time to time she tugged at the hem of her skirt, or self-consciously drew the edges of her neckline together, as though not quite sure that a professor should be showing off so much of her delectable body.

'She'd look a damn sight better naked,' observed the Master under his breath.

Andreas was already imagining her bare breasts bouncing jauntily as she danced on the beach at Rio, clad in nothing but a thin coating of fresh mango juice. It was more than a red-blooded male could stand. 'Er . . . yes. Should I . . . ?'

'A genius, you know,' the Master continued, paying no attention to Hunt. 'A computer genius, a mind that could topple governments if it wanted to. And I could make it want to, Hunt. I could make it want to.'

He had already seen what was coming. 'Master, you're not thinking of initiating her . . . not *here?*'

Le Maitre shook him off like a particularly annoying fruit-fly. 'Ensure that the conference room is empty, and make sure you have the key. We shall add her to our team.'

He walked towards the smiling woman on the stand and Hunt had to stand and watch his own body moving slickly into action. It never had that effect when I owned it, he mused wistfully.

And as though he appreciated the joke, the Master smiled; his teeth glittering sharply under the halogen lights.

Sylvie knew she was dreaming, but this was like no dream she had ever had in her life.

For one thing, she was not herself. She felt much taller, slimmer, more athletic. And she was being whipped with leather, across the back of a leather settee that creaked and juddered with every blow that fell on her bare skin. There was leather all around her. It was leather that was being used to tie her up, leather binding her wrists. A leather strap was round her neck, choking the breath out of her, and there was a leather jacket hooding her eyes. She could smell it, almost taste the tang of tannin and fresh sweat.

A hand pushed her face into the leather, into a pool of still-warm come. It smelt good, and she parted her lips and began to drink thirstily, covering her lips and nose and chin with the white stickiness. A thought kept surfacing again and again in Sylvie's mind. This was so strange; it didn't make sense. This pleasure was intense, the fantasy perfect – but it wasn't *her* fantasy. It was somebody else's. She had always hated leather, and yet she just couldn't help herself. How could that be?

At last every drop of semen was gone. Sylvie purred with delight as the hood slid from her head, letting in the light. A man was standing before her, holding up a leather corset, long leather military boots and a leather truncheon. She almost climaxed at the sight and smell and feel of so much leather, and all for her. Never in her life had she felt so horny, so fulfilled.

I know you, she thought as she looked into the man's face. I know you, though I don't know your name.

The man's name was Alex Carlyle.

The twins came the next night, locking all the doors and pulling down the blinds. In the darkness Sylvie was alone with them, completely at the mercy of their whims.

'Please,' she whimpered as they stripped the clothes from her body. 'Please, I don't know anything.'

The man wrapped her hair around his fist, used

it to draw her towards him, and pushed her to her knees. With his free hand, he unzipped his flies and took out the biggest, hardest penis Sylvie had ever seen. Fully ten inches long, it was so thick a man could scarcely circle it with his fingers.

'Suck my dick.'

She hesitated. His grip on her hair tightened. 'I don't like to be disobeyed, Sylvie. Girls who disobey me have to suffer.'

'You heard him.'

The she-twin thrust two fingers between Sylvie's lips and forced her mouth open. Simultaneously, her brother jerked her face towards his dick and it scythed its way down her throat, so suddenly and so violently that she almost choked.

He growled with satisfaction and started stroking her hair as though she were a favoured pet. 'Take it deeper.'

'I can't!' she tried to splutter, but he silenced her with another hard thrust of his cock that forced his glans against the back of her throat, grazing against the points of her teeth as it passed.

The cat lashed across her bare back with a stinging ferocity that produced a muffled scream, and made Sylvie's body arch with pain.

'Every time you bite your master's dick you will

be punished, do you hear?'

She nodded, blinking away a mist of unshed tears, and began sucking again. He was so big that her jaw-muscles ached, yet with every thrust she could feel herself becoming more and more excited. A terrible hunger had been building up inside her ever since that first time in the shop. It was as if some peculiar virus had infected her body, burning it up with a fever that only sex could assuage.

If she could make him come, if he would only spurt inside her, she felt sure his semen would flow down her throat like a cooling stream, soothing away this terrible, tormenting lust. In her haste to bring him to orgasm, her teeth grazed his flesh and she felt the cat again; but she didn't care about the pain, only about easing this burning need in her belly.

But just as she felt his cock growing even fatter and harder, just as he was surely about to come, he pulled away and pushed her to the floor.

'No, please!'

'Not yet.' The woman dragged her to her knees took her nipples between finger and thumbnail, and squeezed them hard until Sylvie squealed with discomfort. 'You must earn your pleasure.'

'I'll do anything, anything!'

'Goood,' purred the man, pushing the toe of his

boot between her thighs. 'Good girl.' The cold leather pressed ruthlessly against the tender nubbin of Sylvie's clitoris. 'Now tell me what I want to know.'

Sylvie looked up at him. 'I don't understand. Tell you what?'

'She is blocking it out,' observed the male twin.

The woman seized her by the shoulders. 'Leave her to me. Look into my eyes girl, deep into my eyes. Do not resist me.'

The woman's blue eyes seemed to capture hers and hold them prisoner. It was as though all of Sylvie's own will had drained away leaving her at the mercy of this stranger's. She felt dizzy, unstable, floating. And now something else was happening, something even stranger. As she looked into the blue eyes she felt the woman's spirit enter her mind, as easily as walking into a room.

At that precise moment, images surged up unbidden from Sylvie's memory, and began to whirl around her head. Such pain, such terrible pain, like teeth biting into her, stripping the flesh from her bones.

At last all the images died away, leaving only one: the face of Alex Carlyle.

'Who is this man?' demanded the woman's voice,

right next to Sylvie and yet so far away.

'I don't know.'

Something sharp twisted in Sylvie's anus, making her cry out.

'Don't lie to me!'

'I . . . I'm not lying,' panted Sylvie, arse-cheeks clenched tight around the sharp thing that was entering her repeatedly. 'I don't know his name, I . . . he was a stranger, I had sex with him, that's all.'

The image clicked off like the last shot in a slide show, and darkness returned. Only moonlight, dripping into the room through chinks in the blinds, softened the absolute blackness.

'She is not lying,' said the woman, throwing down the corkscrew she had used to bugger the French girl. 'She does not know.'

Her twin contemplated Sylvie, lying in a discarded heap on the floor, as he picked up his black leather gloves and slipped them on. 'Then there is nothing more for us here. Come.'

He took a step towards the door, but Sylvie clutched at him. 'Don't . . . you can't . . .' she gasped. 'Don't leave me like this!'

A gloved hand seized the point of her chin. 'Poor child. Do you remember how it felt when I wore the studded glove? How it felt when I forced it into you and twisted it and gave you no release?'

'Yes!' she sobbed. 'Oh yes!'

'Good.' He smiled thinly. 'Remember it well. For we shall do no more to you until you can tell us that man's name.'

Nothing happened. Absolutely nothing. It was as though the strange events of the past few days had all been a dream, something that had never happened except in Sylvie's own imagination. And yet, her skin still bore the scars, and her poor abandoned body still ached with a need she was powerless to satisfy.

One morning she walked down to the other end of the high street, to fetch a loaf of bread for lunch. Oh, for some decent bread, she thought to herself as she waited her turn in the queue, surveying the miserable array of soggy baguettes and wholemeal loaves so solid you could build a wall out of them. She remembered the little boulangerie at the end of her village street when she was a child; the sweet, buttery aroma of warm croissants that woke you up and told you it was time to go out and buy breakfast . . .

The vision struck her like a bolt from the blue, leaving her no time to see it coming or to resist its sudden, all-consuming power. And it was more than a vision, for she wasn't just seeing it, she was living it.

He was there again, the nameless man who had fucked her on the desk in Tante Mireille's shop. And he was fucking her again, only this time she wasn't Sylvie Montana any more, she was some other woman, some stranger she had never met before in her life.

This is impossible, she told herself. You can't just snap into some other woman's body and start living her life; and yet it was happening, and there was nothing she could do to fight it. And she knew that this other woman had wild red hair and wide green eyes, for she caught glimpses of them in the reflective surfaces: the glass, the chrome, the polished tiles.

Where was she? Who was she? She knew only that the need in her was strong, as strong and urgent as a starving man's need for food. She felt the man's body against hers, hot and hard through her thin cotton dress. His dick was hard and she rubbed her pubis against it and knew that she wanted it inside her, right now.

He grabbed her and they fell sideways. There was chilled whipped cream and confectioner's custard underneath them, between them, slithering over their bodies as they writhed like eels on the floor, soaking through their clothes, plastering their faces and their hair.

She looked up and there was crushed pastry, flaky like snow, fluttering down onto her face. He laughed and squashed great handfuls of cold, red berries onto her breasts. She put out her tongue and licked his lips, and they were hot and sweet and sticky.

The next thing she knew, he pinned her down, threw her soaked skirts over her head and tore down her knickers. Something very cold and smooth trickled down her belly, over her mossy Mound of Venus and into the warm, aromatic softness between her thighs. Cream . . . mousse . . . ice cream, what did it matter? It felt divine.

He rode her amid the mess of fruit and cream and crème anglaise, ripping open her dress and licking fresh crushed strawberries from her nipples. She moaned and begged him to fuck her faster. When he pushed the nozzle of the aerosol can into her cunt and filled her with whipped cream, she knew she was in heaven.

Something ice-cold broke through into her consciousness, and the shock was so great that the spell was instantly broken.

'Are you all right, miss?'

To her absolute horror, Sylvie found herself lying on the floor of the baker's shop in Laverton-on-the-Water, looking up at a crowd of giggling customers and a shop-assistant with half a bottle of sparkling mineral water in her hand.

'I . . .' She sat up and realised that she was dripping wet and freezing cold. The mineral water had soaked right through her blouse, and it was clinging to her braless breasts, making it embarrassingly obvious that her nipples were hard and erect. Oh my God, she thought. What's happening to me? What is this thing that's taking over my life?

'Should I call a doctor?' demanded the assistant.

'No!' exclaimed Sylvie, horrified at the very idea. Scrabbling to her feet, she shouldered her way through the huddle of shoppers and headed for the door.

'Miss . . . miss, you forgot your bread!'

She did not turn round. She just ran and kept on running.

5

From the diary of Andreas Hunt

I am not going to watch. The bastard can make me
stay in the room but he can't make me watch what
he's doing. I just hope he doesn't want me to fuck
her, that's all. I mean, she's a good-looking lass and
all that but necrophilia's definitely not my style.

Oh, yeuch, he's biting her throat now, and I never
could stand the sight of blood. OK, I'm going to try
and think about something else – anything will do.
How about the next instalment of the diary?

Right, where was I? Trying to find Mara, that
was it. So there I am, trying pretty much every damn
trick in the book to find out where she's gone,
because call me big-headed but I'm pretty sure she
wouldn't have left me of her own accord. What I've
got in my trousers may not be a foot long with

multiple pierceings, but I've never had any complaints. Well, not many. Besides, by this point I've started to believe in vampires, and once you're that far gone you'll believe anything.

Eventually I track her to Winterbourne Hall – how's not important and you wouldn't believe it anyway. Turns out the fruitcakes there have got her under mind-control or some such thing, at any rate, she doesn't know what day of the week it is. Which is how she comes to kill me . . .

Hang on Hunt, you're running ahead of yourself here. Back to basics. Winterbourne, hey, what a place. You've never seen anything like it, not even on page three of the *News of the World*. What is it? A kind of Disneyland, I guess, only for perverts. Orgies every night of the week, fresh virgins daily; in short, anything you want, you can get it there. Only snag is, you'll probably wind up dead – or undead, and I'm not sure which is worse.

Anyhow, I manage to lever open one of the downstairs windows and climb in. There's guards all over the place but I dodge them and find my way upstairs, where there are all these incredible, themed sex-rooms. They've all got names on the doors: 'Outer Space', 'Imperial Russia', 'Nero's Palace', just about anything you could dream up in your wildest fantasies.

I come to this door marked 'Orient Express', and in I go, bold as brass. More fool me. Inside, it's all done out like an old-time railway sleeping compartment, all polished brass and old leather. And there's this well-stacked babe in a low-cut black Victorian frock with a veil over her face. Turns out I'm supposed to be the guard and she's the passenger who's lost her ticket. Split-crotch bloomers, a nice round arse – you can guess the rest. I mean, S&M's not really my bag, but when the girl offers you her backside and begs you to punish her, you're not going to disappoint her, are you?

That pink frilly parasol looked really cute sticking out of her cunt like that. And when I fucked her I thought I'd died and gone to heaven. Trouble was, I was so wrapped up in how good it was feeling that I let my guard drop. Next thing I know, she's turned into a spitting vampire Fury and she's trying to sink her gleaming canines into my jugular. Good job I was Runcorn Area Under Thirteens' boxing champion; a swift uppercut to the chin and she was out cold on the couchette.

Naturally, I leg it, and when I get outside I can hear a load of peculiar noises floating up from below. A long way below, like they're coming from the basement or something. I think, maybe that's where they're keeping Mara prisoner, I'd better go down there and check it out.

Bad move.

Now, I know you're going to think this a load of bollocks, but you've got to believe me. As soon as I started walking down those steps into the cellars, I could feel the evil in the place. Ancient, evil energy, reaching out to grab me, like there was this big black claw of a hand dragging me on when all I really wanted was to get the hell out of there. But Andreas Hunt, the *Comet*'s number one investigative hack, never ran out on a story in his life; besides which, I wasn't about to leave Mara there with all those crazies.

I could hear chanting, and people shrieking with laughter; and as I turned the corner in the staircase I walked right into the middle of something out of Hieronymus Bosch. Writhing, naked bodies, smeared with something sticky and red that looked suspiciously like blood; faces contorted with lust; people fucking and buggering each other, sucking cocks, flaying each other with whips. And right in the middle of it all, a massive stone sarcophagus that could have been lifted straight out of Tutankhamun's tomb. I couldn't see into it, but somehow I knew what was inside. A man, four thousand years old, trapped inside a flawless block of crystal. I could feel the evil emanating from his cold, dead eyes . . .

And then I saw Mara. Stark naked, except for the crystal pendant that swung between her breasts – and the crystal dagger in her hands.

I shouted out to her: 'Mara . . . come with me, quickly!'

She turned her face towards me, but I could tell from the look in her eyes that she was drugged, or hypnotised or something. She didn't look at me; she looked right through me.

'Mara!'

She started walking towards me, and – call me naive – I thought I'd got through to her. What I didn't understand was that the man in the crystal was controlling her, using her body like a puppet to get what he wanted. And what he wanted right now was my body.

And I don't mean in the Biblical sense.

A sound snapped Andreas out of his reverie. The dead woman on the floor of the conference room was stirring. There were two neat puncture marks on her bare throat, but she did not seem at all inconvenienced by having lost every drop of blood in her body.

'Master,' she sighed blissfully, opening her eyes.

The Master smiled and extended a hand for her to kiss. 'Rise, slave.'

She got to her feet a little unsteadily, her skirt still up round her waist, her thighs still wet with semen. A thin trickle of congealed blood ran like a sword-slash down the sleeve of her tight white blouse.

'How may I serve you, Master?'

He looked deep into her eyes and clicked his fingers. And Professor daCosta began to dance for her new master, moving to a sexual samba that he and he alone had composed. Her sleek hips swayed, her cherry-red nipples quivered under the thin white fabric, and she closed her eyes, smiling the secret smile of a fallen angel as she began to caress her own breasts.

The Master threw back his head and laughed Andreas Hunt's laugh. It was the scariest thing Andreas had ever heard.

Sylvie needed help, and she knew it. The visions were becoming more frequent and even more overpowering. How long would it be before she was completely unable to control herself?

She hesitated a long time on the steps of the parish church, then went inside. It was a long time since she had been inside a church, let alone consulted a priest, and she wouldn't have been doing it now if things hadn't been so desperate.

It was a very old church, and the walls were so thick that scarcely any of the June warmth penetrated the butter-yellow stones. The atmosphere inside was cool and dark, yet Sylvie could still feel the hunger burning inside her, the flame low but threatening to flare up at any moment.

'Father?'

The figure of a middle-aged man emerged from behind the rood screen, quite tall but hunched about the shoulders and with thinning, mud-brown hair. His black cassock was several inches too short for him, and swung around his ankles, revealing unfashionable grey trousers and black shoes that had seen better days.

'Ah – Miss Montana?' She nodded. 'They told me you wished to see me. A personal matter, I understand?'

'It's very embarrassing . . . I'm not even sure you'll believe me, but I couldn't think of anyone else to talk to.'

'That's all right, my dear. Whatever it is, I'm sure you won't shock me.'

Sylvie wasn't so sure, but let him sit her down on the font pew and settle himself beside her, hands neatly folded on his lap. He listened intently as she described what had been happening to her.

'Visions, you say?'

'Sexual visions, Father. Terrible visions. It's as if I'm inside the body of this man, and I am seeing and feeling what he is doing to . . . to all these women . . .' She licked her dry lips and stared down at the flor, deeply uncomfortable in the presence of this completely asexual priest.

'He is having sexual relations with them?'

'Yes, Father. All kinds of sex, violent sometimes. I don't want this to happen to me, but there is nothing I can do to stop it. Please help me, I don't know where else to turn.'

The priest seemed reassuringly unruffled. He scratched behind his ear. 'Well, well. How very upsetting for you. I don't have much experience in these matters of course, but I suppose it could be a form of possession . . .'

'You think I am possessed! By evil spirits!'

He patted her hand. 'Please, don't upset yourself. I'm sure it's nothing serious. And as it happens, I may just be able to help you.'

A great rush of relief washed over her. 'You can?'

'Not myself, you understand, I'm just a doddery old churchman. But I do know of someone . . . a man called Hunt.'

'Hunt?' She shook her head. The name meant nothing to her.

'Andreas Hunt.' The priest searched in the folds of his cassock and produced a pencil and a scrap of paper. 'Friend of a friend, he often investigates strange happenings. He helped us out once with a haunting we had . . .'

'Thank you. Thank you, Father.'

'Don't mention it, my dear. Now, if you'll excuse me, I have one or two other matters I must attend to.'

He watched her walk back down the nave, push open the heavy oak door, and heard it swing shut behind her. Then he turned, dissolved slowly into a transparent silhouette, and stepped right through the church wall.

Alex sat on a Queen Anne chair at his workbench, contemplating the jewelled box. It contemplated him back, apparently untroubled by the knowledge of its own power.

Quite simply, he had never known a week like this last one. Since that first dazzling success with the leather queen, he had grown increasingly bold and adventurous. His willing victims had offered themselves to him one after the other, and one after the other he had had them all.

Fondly he recalled the big-breasted redhead in the patisserie. all those crushed strawberries dripping down the front of her dress. Then the wide-mouthed Indian girl who sold retro clothing and looked so heart-stoppingly horny in that pink Fifties corselette. Not to mention the complete stranger who'd just happened to be posting a letter in the box outside his workshop. So many, he'd practically lost count.

And still he wanted more, ever more.

A loud rapping on the workshop door broke his concentration.

'Hi, Alex.'

A head of platinum blonde curls appeared round the door. It was the carpenter who rented the workshop next door.

'Hi, Karen. What can I do for you?'

She stepped inside. Karen was fortyish but boy was she well-preserved. He'd never really thought of her as his type before, but now he came to look at her properly he had to admit that older women had their charms. Alex found his eyes travelling over her plumply rounded curves, and lingering rather longer than strictly necessary on the straining buttons of her red checked work shirt. He speculated on the breaking stress of reinforced button-thread. Just how big were her breasts? Forty-two, forty-four? Forty-six double-D and still counting?

She waved a finger in the air. 'Splinter.'

'Ah.' He forced himself to sound sympathetic and hoped she hadn't noticed him staring at her chest.

'It's gone right in and I can't see it to get it out. Don't suppose you've got anything here I can ... ?' Her eyes lighted on the jewelled box, lying open on the workbench, and the tiny magnifying glass attached by its fine gold chain. 'Ooh, that's pretty. What is it?'

'Oh, nothing. Just a worthless bit of old tat. Amazing what you can do with coloured glass and a bit of gold plate.'

Without warning, Karen pounced. 'Aha, magnifying glass, just what I need.'

Before he could say 'I'd really rather you didn't', she was reaching out for the glass. He went for it at the exact same moment and their hands touched.

Oh, hell, no, thought Alex as panic gripped him and a white mist began to swirl and curl out of the open box. It's not supposed to happen like this; I'm supposed to be in control.

He peeped gingerly into the box. As expected, it was showing Karen, but there was no sign of the usual DMs or the glue-smeared cargo pants. She was completely naked, her magnificent breasts bobbing like two huge pink clouds above plump hips and creamy thighs. Naked men knelt at her feet like balding cherubs as she strode by, licking her thighs, kissing her feet, pleading with her to piss in their unworthy mouths. But she just smiled at them indulgently and went on pushing the big, shiny coach-built pram. The pram with Alex in it.

He shuddered with suppressed desire as she kissed the tip of her finger and pressed it to his lips. She was smiling, utterly spaced-out, exactly the way the antique shop girl had been, that day in Laverton-on-the-Water. She stroked his cheek lovingly.

'Is baby hungry? Does baby want his feed?'

A terrible surge of need coursed through Alex's body and he nodded mutely, helplessly, a prisoner of the box and its twenty-twenty vision. Karen began unbuttoning her shirt, filling him with such suspenseful excitement that his chest ached with the effort of forcing himself to breathe.

'That's right, baby, Mummy's getting her titties out for you. You like Mummy's titties, don't you?'

Underneath the red and white check cotton she was wearing the biggest, most sensible-looking bra Alex had ever seen. It was made of white, double-sewn cotton, with broad straps that strained to hold the weight of her firm, melon-sized breasts. He shivered as she released a tiny Velcro strip and the left cup peeled away, revealing creamy-white flesh marbled with fine blue veins, and a large, puckered nipple haloed with fine brown hairs.

'Baby come to Mummy,' she breathed, and pulled him towards her. 'Come and suck on Mummy's nipple. You know it gets her all excited, don't you?'

Her flesh enveloped him like the softest, dreamiest pillow. She smelt of talc and fresh, piney wood shavings, and something sweeter that he recognised instantly yet could not put a name to. It was only when she pushed her nipple between his parted lips that he realised what it was, and felt the orgasmic spurt of warm milk on his tongue.

'Good baby, clever baby,' she cooed, as she pushed his hand inside her big, mumsy knickers. 'Now find Mummy's g-spot; and if you're a very good boy perhaps Mummy will let you fuck her.'

* * *

The country might be in turmoil following the sudden death of the Prime Minister, but it was business as usual at Winterbourne.

In the Great Hall, which had been redecorated in an opulent Napoleonic style presaging the coming of the Master's new Empire of Lust, the faithful were at their devotions. Suspended from the ceiling in ornate gilded cages, pretty youths danced, their nipples, lips and penises pierced with heavy crystals that caught the light from a thousand blazing candles.

Beside the sunken pool, vampire sluts lounged on gold and purple cushions, each taking her turn to satisfy the Hall's latest 'guests'. Among the most recently initiated of the sluts was Professor daCosta, blindfolded and dressed only in spike-heeled boots and a white satin corset laced to fourteen inches at the waist, displaying her naked breasts and rounded arse to perfection.

It was every new initiate's task to learn her craft thoroughly, so that she might serve her Master and provide him with the sexual energy he needed to grow strong; and the Professor was not proving to be a disappointment. Already she had been buggered by Heimdal, the Master's henchman, and by

Ibrahim, the massively-endowed Ethiopian, and now she was on her knees by the pool, taking two cocks in her pussy while licking out the vampire slut Anastasia Dubois.

'An apt pupil, Master,' commented Heimdal, offering LeMaitre a goblet of aphrodisiac wine from a golden tray. 'She will soon be able to serve us well in the world.'

'Indeed.'

'There is a new virgin, Master. Barely seventeen years old and fresh as a rosebud. Would you like the boy brought to you now? I am assured he has a delightfully tight arsehole.'

'Do not bother me with such trivialities!' snapped the Master, dashing away the tray of wine. 'There are far more pressing matters demanding my attention.'

Heimdal bowed. 'Yes, Master; forgive me, Master.' He took the bullwhip from his belt and lashed it across Dolores daCosta's back, making her squeal and arch her spine.

'You. Slut.'

She kissed the ground before him. 'Lord Heimdal?'

'Clean up this mess.' He twisted the heavy chain which divided into two parts, each attached to one of her nipple-rings; and she gasped with exquisite pain. 'And if you miss a single drop, you will be severely punished.'

'Yes, Lord Heimdal. At once, Lord Heimdal.' Putting out her tongue, she began to lap up the spilt wine.

Steepling his fingers, the Master sat back. Beneath him, his throne of naked bodies writhed and copulated, offering up the worship of their lust to him.

'Continue,' he said curtly. 'And this time, tell me what I want to hear.'

The twins stood before him, hand in hand and still defiant. Though loyal to the Master, they could not be so easily cowed, perhaps because they shared a double strength, a knowledge that they were two halves of a greater whole.

'It was impossible,' began the male twin, 'because she . . .'

'. . . truly did not have the answer,' cut in his sister. 'And when we . . .'

'. . . tortured her with pleasure, she was unable . . .'

'. . . to tell us this man's name.'

The Master's expression was growing increasingly thunderous. 'Nothing is impossible, *nothing*, do you understand?'

Two identical pairs of eyes returned his gaze. This time, the female twin spoke first.

'Master, we are confident that she will . . .'

'. . . discover the name, because . . .'

'. . . without it, she knows that there will be no more pleasure . . .'

'. . . or pain.'

The Master dug his fingernails into a bare, thrusting torso beneath him. 'I will have that box, do you understand?'

'Yes, Master.'

'Soon I shall run this country openly, not merely by stealth as I do now. But then our task will only be beginning; for it is then that I must confront the true powers of this world: the Templars, the Japanese techno-demons, the Immortal African Goddess, the Illuminati . . . all of them. If I have the box – *when* I have the box – my task will be so much simpler. It will extend the range of my astral vision even into the souls of those who are psychically strong and believe they can resist me.

'I shall have all I have ever desired. And swiftly.'

The slut who was known as Taz listened closely. It was not easy, for she was part of the Master's throne and there were cocks in her sex, her arse,

her throat. But she sensed that this was both
interesting and important.

Yes, she told herself. Christian would be very
interested in this.

6

From the diary of Andreas Hunt

I'm sitting in my room at Winterbourne Hall. My private room. It has everything a discerning bloke could want in a whorehouse: waterbed, cupboard full of sex toys, hot and cold running vampire sluts . . . Great, if you don't mind shagging something that might turn round and rip your throat out. To be honest, there's only one woman who pushes all my buttons, and that's Mara Fleming.

She's lying asleep on the bed. Not surprising she's knackered, all things considered. I mean, these Roman orgies take it out of you, and that Heimdal's a head-case. When he plays Caligula you just know the horse is going to be a real one. Plus, you have to put everything you've got into playing the slave or the gladiator or whatever, otherwise pretty damn soon somebody's going to twig that you're not a vampire after all, you're the Master's mortal enemy.

Hell but she makes me horny, lying there like that, all sprawled out on her back with her auburn hair trailing over her shoulder and her right breast. Her red-gold pubic curls are wet with semen, and her pussy-lips are swollen like fat pink petals. We've been through a lot together, since she gave me that Tarot reading on Whitby prom and a stiffy the size of Blackpool Tower.

She smiles and rolls onto her side, and I can see red scratches running down her flanks, the marks of sharp little teeth up the inside of her thighs. How many sex-hungry lovers took her, there in the Great Hall? Is she dreaming about them or is she fantasising about me? Silly question.

Anyhow, like I was saying, I was right about her being at Winterbourne Hall. There I am, standing at the top of the cellar steps, shouting at her to come with me and get the hell out of it, and she's standing there stark naked, kind of looking right through me, like her mind's not her own any more. She was still well screwable, though, even with magic symbols painted all over her body in fresh blood.

I can feel the power from the dead man in the block of crystal; and all at once I get this horrible feeling that he isn't dead at all – or at least, his body may be but his spirit sure isn't. In fact, he's controlling everything. I know I ought to turn tail and run, but I don't. I can't tell you why, I mean, I've never seen myself as Sir Galahad, only I just can't just run off and leave her there, can I? It's obvious they're about to do something horrible to her.

I walk down the steps. Amazingly, nobody makes a move to stop me. They just go on fucking each other like the world's going to end and this is their last chance to act out all the dirty pictures they've downloaded off the Internet. Mara's standing by the sarcophagus. I walk towards her. It's only then I notice she's got this crystal dagger in her hands and – oh, shit – she's pointing it right at my chest.

So she kills me, right? Don't switch off, I'm not a nutter, listen. She doesn't know what she's doing, but she stabs me through the heart and technically speaking I'm dead, right? Only I'm not. And believe me, nobody's more surprised than I am when I realise I've just switched places with the bloke in the coffin.

That's right. He's poncing around in my body, telling everybody he's the Master and he's going to shag the world, and me? I'm trapped in his foetid, four-thousand-year-old corpse, in a sodding big block of stone. In short, I'm worse than dead, I'm fucked.

And that was just the beginning.

Sylvie sat in reception at *Mondo Bizarro*, trying not to stare at the man with two noses. She had started out thinking that the vicar was wrong; her story was way too weird for anyone to believe. But maybe not. This was, after all, the magazine that had published exclusive pictures of Genghis Khan, working as a turf accountant in Tooting.

She'd tried hard to find Andreas Hunt, the man the vicar had told her about, but it was an old address and nobody seemed to know where he'd gone. It was Hunt's former editor at the *Comet* who'd told her about Greg Usher. Mind you, he hadn't been very complimentary: the words 'prick' and 'moron' stuck particularly clearly in the mind.

Sylvie crossed and uncrossed her legs nervously, watched with interest by a fat man in the open-plan office beyond. Self-consciously she tugged at the hem of her skirt. She hoped that wasn't him; he was all slobbery, with rolls of flesh spilling over the waistband of trousers two sizes too small and dandruff on the shoulders of his orange shirt.

A small-breasted vixen strode past on high-heeled Prada mules: 'Tell Clive editorial meeting at three-thirty, or his balls are mine,' she snapped over her shoulder, tapping irritably away towards a distant door in a cloud of *Tendre Poison*.

'Right you are, Cindy,' trilled the receptionist, waiting a couple of seconds before adding 'stuck-up cow'. She looked over the edge of the desk at Sylvie. 'Want another coffee?'

'No thanks.'

'Booked your holidays yet?'

'Well, actually . . .'

'Me and Tray are going to Benidorm. Can't wait to get out of this place; load of bleeding weirdos, if you ask me.'

A face appeared round the corner. It belonged to a tall, youngish man with dark, slightly wavy hair, a day's growth of stubble and a long, slightly crooked nose that had never quite recovered from a particularly vicious fourth-form rugby lesson. He wasn't exactly good-looking, thought Sylvie, but if he was ugly at least he was ugly in an interesting way.

'You're looking nice today, Charlene.'

The receptionist preened her expensively tousled locks. 'Ta very much.'

'I always did like lurex boob-tubes. I mean, they never go out of fashion really, do they?' The young man leaned over the desk and turned the visitors' book towards him. 'Somebody to see me, is there?'

Charlene pointed a blue fingernail at Sylvie. 'Her. She's foreign,' she added in a tone that implied 'and mentally defective with it'.

'Oh, right.' Greg turned his gaze on Sylvie, flicked a currant off his tie and switched on a schoolboy smile. 'Hi. My name's Greg.'

'Sylvie. Sylvie Montana.'

He stuck out his hand and she took it. The moment their flesh touched, Sylvie could feel something flash between them; a spark of sensual electricity that told her this was going to be more than just a casual conversation.

'So, what can I do for you . . . er . . . Sylvie? If it's topless modelling for the voodoo feature . . .'

'Actually, no, I wanted to talk to you about something that has happened to me. Something very strange. And . . . er . . . embarrassing.'

Usher's eyebrows lifted a fraction. 'I see. Well, why don't we go into the interview room? We'll be more private in there.' He waved a hand in Charlene's direction. 'Rustle us up some coffee and biscuits, will you?'

The receptionist raised a single blue-tipped finger. 'Rustle it up your frigging self.'

The door of the interview room closed behind them and Sylvie found herself sitting on one end of a red sofa, under a picture of a turnip that looked like Bart Simpson. Greg Usher perched himself in front of her, on the edge of the coffee table.

'So. This thing you wanted to talk to me about.'

She felt her throat tighten. 'It's . . . it's very difficult for me. You see, it is all about . . . sex.'

The smile on Greg's face grew perceptibly broader. 'Really? Bit of a scandal brewing, is there? Don't tell me – another bishop with a taste for bondage. Well, don't worry.' He patted her knee. 'I'm very discreet. And we pay well,' he added as an extra inducement.

'No, nothing like that.' Usher was behaving like an overgrown schoolboy, thought Sylvie; by rights she ought not to fancy him at all. But there was something about him . . . something that stirred the fire smouldering in her belly and made her labia ache with secret need. Could he feel it too? 'Actually, it is about a . . . a box.'

Usher's brow furrowed. 'What kind of box?'

'Gold, encrusted with jewels. It . . . it makes people do things. It has special . . . powers.'

Greg scratched his nose. 'Hang on a minute, you've lost me. What do you mean, special powers?'

'You look into it and there is a tiny spy-glass inside. Whoever you see through that glass, it shows you . . . it reveals their secret desires to you, and makes you irresistible to them.'

It all came spilling out: her Tante Mireille's shop, the journal, the stranger who had screwed her on her aunt's old desk and vanished, taking the box with him, the sinister twins, the visions that tormented her aching, lustful body.

The journalist sat in silence for a moment, then his face cracked into a grin and he guffawed. 'Nice one; plot for a porno flick, is it?'

'Sorry?'

'I mean, obviously you're not serious.'

'Serious! Of course I am serious, Monsieur Usher!'

He looked taken aback. 'Come on, Sylvie, you're not really saying you've got some kind of magical box that turns people horny? I'm a journalist. You can't seriously expect me to believe a load of old bollocks like that.'

Tears of anger and despair sprang to Sylvie's dark eyes. 'I come to you in good faith. I have nowhere else to turn since Monsieur Hunt has disappeared. I believe you will help me and you laugh in my face!'

Usher's expression changed. 'Hunt, you say? Not Andreas Hunt?'

She nodded. 'A priest gave me his name, he told me he specialised in investigating strange phenomena. It was Andreas Hunt's editor who gave me your name.'

'Hunt. Well, well, well.' Usher rubbed his stubbly chin. That name just wouldn't go away, every time he tried to forget it it twanged back in his face like an overstretched rubber band.

'I thought you would understand,' said Sylvie accusingly, wiping the back of her hand across her eyes.

Usher searched through his pockets and produced a crumpled tissue. 'Here, wipe your eyes. Look, I'm sorry, I never meant to upset you, it's just . . . well . . . you've got to admit, it all sounds a bit far-fetched.'

'Maybe, but it's true. The box exists.'

'And you've got it now?'

'It was stolen from me. That's why the twins won't leave me alone. I have to find it, Monsieur Usher. You have to help me.'

A box. Usher drummed his fingers thoughtfully on the coffee table. A magical box that made people screw each other. Hadn't he read somewhere about something just like that? A box commissioned by Catherine the Great, to give her sexual power over every man and woman who dared oppose her? Yeah, but maybe this girl had read the same article. All the same, she seemed genuine enough. Maybe she was just plain nuts. At any rate, it didn't stop him fancying her.

'Coffee?' he asked, unsure what to say.

'No thank you.' Sylvie got to her feet. 'Perhaps I had better go, since you do not believe me.'

He caught her by the arm. 'No, you can't go anywhere, not in this state.'

'I will get a taxi back to my hotel.'

'Tell you what.' He sprang up. 'Why don't I go with you? Make sure you get back safely. What do you say?'

It was more than she could take. Sitting next to him in the black cab as it wove its way in and out of the traffic.

Her senses had been heightened ever since that first time, in the shop. She could smell his desire, and with every breath she took her need grew stronger. Her fingers crept across the seat and touched his leg. Startled, he turned to look at her, and saw the peculiar, dazed expression enter her eyes. It was like looking into the face of a sexed-up sleepwalker.

'Sylvie?'

She did not reply, but he heard her breath becoming more and more hoarse. Her hand grew bolder, sliding under his jacket and across his lap until they met the hardening bulge under his pants. He let out a soft gasp as she grasped his dick through the fabric and dug her nails hard into the flesh. Bloody hell, what had got into the woman? His eyes flicked towards the driver, but he was too busy yelling obscenities out of the open window to notice the girl unzipping Greg Usher's pants and slowly sliding down until her hair cascaded over his lap and her soft mouth closed tight about his throbbing shaft.

It was the most amazing afternoon Greg had ever had – and when you worked on *Mondo Bizarro* you soon grew accustomed to the unexpected. It didn't end when they reached the hotel, either. True, the doorman gave them a knowing look as she practically dragged Usher across the lobby, but the journalist didn't give a shit what he might think. As the lift doors closed on them, she lifted her skirts and offered her backside to him, and he watched himself screwing her in the mirrored walls, from every angle you could imagine.

The room had a balcony that overlooked the tube station. If the thousands of commuters streaming past had bothered to look up, they would have seen the best free show in London: a bosomy, dark-haired girl leaning over the rail with her bare tits hanging down, and a bloke giving it to her up the arse like his life depended on it.

Yeah, it was quite an afternoon. And it wasn't even Greg Usher's birthday.

This time, Alex was well-prepared. This time it would be sweet, whatever it turned out to be. He knew now where he'd gone wrong, that last time. He should never have let Karen touch the glass; he'd lost control of the fantasy and there was no way he was going through that again. He only wished it hadn't felt so good.

He pushed the embarrassing memory to the back of his mind and concentrated on the present. Sandi was going to be the perfect lay, he could feel it in his blood. Tall, lithe, naturally blonde . . . and where her legs stopped, her tits began. The fact was, he'd had the hots for her ever since she sold him the lease on his flat but, despite repeated seduction attempts, he'd never got anywhere with her. She only went for the hairy bodybuilder type, that was the trouble. Alex smirked. Well, all that was going to change tonight.

He checked his watch and lit the scented candles. Almost seven-thirty; she'd be here soon. On the pretext that he'd decided to sell up, Sandi had agreed to come round and see him, and he was waiting for her. Oh, yes, he was waiting all right – and so was the box.

'Hi,' she said in her husky voice as she sort of slithered into his hallway, her supermodel curves shown off to perfection in a short, clingy white dress and stockings that shimmered in the candlelight. 'Ready to talk business?'

'You took the words right out of my mouth. Drink?'

'Later, maybe.' She was cool and businesslike, and it just made him madder for her than ever. 'First, I want to look over the flat.'

He caught her with the spy-glass as she bent over to look at his collection of African fetishes. And lo and behold, there Sandi was in all her glory: doggy-style on a bridal four-poster, wedding-dress up round her waist and getting it up the arse. He'd never have imagined that that was her bag, but now he could see how she was going to squirm with pleasure on the end of his dick, Alex simply couldn't wait.

He knew the box would already have brought the fantasy into her mind. All he had to do was bring it to life.

'Why don't you come and take a look at the bedroom with me? I was wondering if a four-poster might fit in there . . .'

He saw the glint in her eye and went in for the kill as she was standing by the bed. Sliding a hand onto her firm, round bum, he murmured: 'You know something, Sandi? I could really go for you in a wedding dress.'

'Oh, really?'

He elaborated. 'A big white frilly one, lots of lace. Stockings and suspenders underneath, a little blue garter . . .'

She smiled and kissed him. Then her fingers started walking down the front of his shirt, flicking open the buttons. He growled softly as she unzipped him and released his dick, blessing the day he'd walked into that girl's shop and nicked her old desk.

'You're hard,' Sandi breathed. 'But not hard enough for me. We'll have to do something about that, won't we?'

I've died and gone to heaven, thought Alex as

her supple fingers worked away at his shaft, smearing the ooze of lubricating fluid from its bulbous tip right down to the balls, coating it with a glass-smooth finish that made her hand slide over it with tantalising lightness.

Just when he thought she had driven him to the point of no return, she got to her knees and began to suck his balls. Her mouth was large and warm and deliciously wet, and he began to shiver with unsuppressed excitement as her teeth teased the juicy fruit. Alex could feel the spunk gathering, but knew she would not let him come until he was inside her, the way she wanted him to be.

She ran her tongue along the underside of his shaft, and smiled up at him. 'I bet you can't guess what I want now.'

'I bet I can.'

'All right, then, why don't you go right ahead and give it to me?'

He took her in his arms and threw her onto the bed, face-down, sliding his hands under her skirt and pushing aside the gusset of her panties. His teeth bit into her backside and she flexed her hips, pushing her bum-cheeks into his hands, offering herself to him.

It was an offer he couldn't refuse. Her buttocks

parted so sweetly, revealing a tiny puckered hole the colour of raw amber. It was incredibly tight, but he was so hard and wet that he slid into her as sweetly as a warm spoon cutting through whipped cream.

'Oh yes,' she moaned. 'Oh yes, oh *yes*!'

He felt for her breasts as he buggered her, loving their unusual firmness in his hands, squeezing them through the firm, lacy bra that held everything in check. She was loving it, but he knew there was something she would love even more. And his right hand slipped round to the front of her panties, gliding down inside . . .

Which was the moment when Alex Carlyle got the shock of his life.

Sylvie awoke from her trance with a start.

For a moment she did not know where she was, only that she was in the open air and her bare arms were cold, and there were a lot of people standing and staring at her.

'Bloody hell,' repeated Greg Usher, taking a couple of steps backwards.

The memory flooded back. She was a blonde woman, a blonde woman in a wedding dress. Sylvie looked down at herself and realised what she had just been doing. Her skirt was up round her waist, and she had been rubbing her backside against the rough bark of a horse chestnut tree – right in the middle of Green Park.

She reddened. Greg edged a little further away. 'What the hell do you think you're doing, Sylvie?'

Another memory sprang into her mind. Suddenly panicking, she placed a hand on her crotch – and breathed a sigh of relief. It was OK. She'd only been *dreaming* that she had a penis. Well, at least that was one less thing to worry about.

'He said he must have it,' said Taz, eagerly. She was kneeling on the floor of Christian's kitchen, naked save for her slave-collar and the spiked ivory butt-plug he allowed her to wear when she had pleased him. 'He said it would enable him to defeat the secret powers who rule the world, I swear he did.'

'Silence, slave.' Christian drove another staple through a hole in her nipple and she whimpered with pleasure. 'I need to think.' He paced up and down, in front of the drawn-down blind. 'Well, well. Nobody told me the box was *that* important . . .'

He spun round, the staple gun still in his hand. The vampire slut followed it with her eyes, silently pleading for just a little more pain.

'You have done well,' he concluded. 'Come, slave, you shall have your reward.'

Her undead eyes sparkled with gratitude as he threw her into the chest freezer, locked down the lid and walked away.

7

From the diary of Andreas Hunt

So there I am, trapped in this dead bloke's corpse, embedded in a sodding big block of stone, while the Master's parading round Winterbourne in my body – yes, *my* body – snacking on twenty fresh virgins a day.

Unfair, I call it. I really liked that body. *And* I'd just paid out to have my crowns redone.

Anyhow, by this time Mara's snapped out of the mind-control thing, and she's feeling pretty shitty about what's happened. Face it, who wouldn't? Not only have you just stabbed your ace reporter boyfriend through the heart, you've also unleashed a force of pure, erotic evil on the world. Not bad for one day's work. So straight away she sets about trying to get me out of the crystal and back into my body (and hers, if you get my drift, heh, heh). Sorry, where was I? Oh, yes. Ahem.

The thing is, while I'm silently screaming to be let out and getting nowhere, Mara gets caught up in this plan the Master's got to steal the mummified penis of Osiris. No, don't ask, it's too bloody complicated. Let's just say if you were to get your hands on that particular twelve inches, you could wave goodbye to Viagra *and* raise your girlfriend from the dead. Cool, huh?

'Trouble is, like everything always does, it goes pear-shaped; and the next thing Mara knows, the Master's queen, Sedet, has nicked her body and (I hope you're concentrating, I'll be testing you on this later), Mara's soul's been forced into the body of vampire slut Anastasia Dubois.

Fortunately it's a nice body, red hair, really big bazookas, just my kind of thing. In fact, I can't say I've any major objections to the new-look Mara, but it's a bit of a downer for her. Can't be much fun playing the Master's undead sex-slut when you're a white witch with a moral objection to ripping people's throats out. Still, she's a brainy lass and somehow she gets by; and better than that, she starts channelling all the sexual energies from the whorehouse into my spirit, strengthening it for the day she finds a way to get me out of the crystal . . .

Mara walked in from the bathroom, wearing nothing but her crystal body-piercings and the tiniest of white towels. Her body still steamed from the hot shower, and tiny water droplets glistened on the auburn tangle of her public curls, just visible beneath the hem of the towel.

'So,' she smiled, letting the towel fall to the floor, 'which of my bodies do you prefer?'

Andreas pressed his mouth against her belly, and scented droplets trickled onto his tongue. He breathed in the perfume of her, hot and musky and sweet.

'Hmm, good question.' He got up from the bed and walked around her, like Arthur Negus examining a particularly nice chest of drawers. 'Good arse.' He gave it a proprietorial squeeze. 'Mind you, the other one was nice too. 'Course, when it comes to arses I always say you can never have too much.'

Mara's lips twitched. 'Sophisticate.'

'Too right. And then there's your tits.'

'Naturally.' She cupped them in her two hands, so that the long, dusky-pink stalks of her nipples protruded between the gaps in her fingers. 'So what do you reckon, then? These or the others?'

Andreas took a nipple into his mouth and teased it with the tip of his tongue. It hardened instantly, and so did he. 'Mmm,' he murmured, reluctantly allowing it to escape. 'You ask such difficult questions.'

'What about my thighs, then?' enquired Mara, putting his hands on them and sliding them up the silken inner surface, flawlessly smooth with just a hint of muscle.

Andreas growled. 'Bloody fantastic.' His fingers slid to the utterly irresistible zone where thigh became pussy. 'God, but you make me horny.'

Laughing, she pushed his hands away. 'Hang on, you still haven't told me which you prefer – the old me or the new me.'

'How about both?' he suggested hopefully.

'Come on, choose!'

'I'm not sure,' teased Andreas, pushing the side of his hand between Mara's outer labia, releasing a flood of sweet, slippery juices. 'Why don't you remind me how good this one is?'

He thought he was in control but, as usual, he was wrong. As he pushed her down onto the bed, she rolled over and took the initiative, straddling him playfully with those strong, irresistibly smooth thighs.

'Remember what I used to do? With these?' She ran her hands over the skin, still pink from the shower and glossy with rose-scented cream.

Andreas's grin spread so wide, the top of his head threatened to fall off. 'What? You mean . . . ?'

'Uh-huh.'

'You haven't done that in ages.'

'Maybe I should remind you how good it feels.'

As her thighs closed about his dick, imprisoning it with such tender ruthlessness that Andreas knew he'd never ask for parole, he understood that the question was meaningless.

Old body or new, he didn't give a tinker's cuss. It was still Mara. And she still made his dick throb like nobody else ever could.

Alex was having a hard time, in more ways than one.

He'd tried like crazy to blot Sandi out of his mind, only it wasn't that easy. Frankly, he had a horrible suspicion he was never going to forget sucking another man's cock, and everything that followed on from it – and, worst of all, *enjoying* the experience.

He groaned. What was happening to him? What the hell was happening? The box knew, but it wasn't offering him any answers. He fidgeted with it, turning it this way and that, trying to see it as just a lump of gold with a few precious stones stuck to it. An expensive but vulgar trinket, that was all it was. Sell it; no, even better, melt it down. Then it would be out of his life for ever, and into somebody else's. Only he had the weirdest feeling that it would not be that simple.

Resolved to sort the thing out once and for all the next day, he unlocked the safe and put the box inside with the money he'd got for the old desk. With the door locked and the key safely in his wallet, he ought to have felt better, but he didn't. It was as if the safe door was made of glass, for all the use it was. Even with an inch of steel between him and it, he could see the box in his mind's eye, as clear as day. He could turn his back on it and walk away, but its image would still follow him, mocking him, burning into his helpless soul.

Quite simply, he couldn't leave the damned thing alone. Slipping the key out of his wallet, he unlocked the safe with trembling fingers and removed the box. He could have sworn it exuded a peculiar, pulsing warmth, like the body of some beautiful but malevolent creature. He was both drawn to it and repelled by it, dreading looking at it because he knew it would make him open the lid again and take out the little spy-glass . . .

No. He couldn't pass this on to someone else. Alex had never been an altruistic kind of guy, and God knows how much money he was passing up, but however much it was, it wasn't enough. There was only one thing he could do with this box, and he had to do it right this minute.

Go straight down to Hyde Park and chuck it in the Serpentine.

It was early morning and he was quite alone.

Alex stood at the water's edge, gazing down at his own reflection, and the image of the box in his hands. This is it, he told himself. This is finally it. One good throw and I'm rid of it forever.

He swallowed hard, trying not to think of all the women he could have had, or the price it could have fetched. Telling himself that the thing was cursed, that in the end nothing but bad things could ever come out of it. Almost convinced, he drew his arm back, wondering if at the final moment he would really be able to persuade his fingers to let go.

Then he saw her. The early-morning runner. Not

just any runner, either; this one was a hot black babe in an expensive jogging suit that moulded itself tightly to her young and perfect curves. It was just Alex's luck that she paused for breath, not ten yards away, smiled at him and said 'Hi.'

'Hi.' His throat was so dry and tight, he could hardly get the word out.

'Gonna be a lovely day isn't it?' She had full, moist lips, and those amazing, small firm breasts that only teenagers have: hard as apples, juicy as ripe passion fruit.

'Er . . . yeah. Looks that way.'

Alex tried, God how he tried. But he couldn't help it, he truly couldn't. It was like he was a puppet, and the box held all the strings.

They were in the bushes.

Afterwards, Alex couldn't quite recall the details of how they got there – the details were all fuzzy in his head, like the aftermath of too much alcohol on an empty stomach. But what happened when they got there was engraved in his memory for all eternity.

The ground was dry and dusty, for the most part softly padded with a papery covering of last year's leaves, but spiked here and there by the occasional sharp stone or broken twig. Around and above them, a dense mass of leaves and branches screened them from prying eyes. Or at least, they seemed to; and frankly, at that precise moment, Alex was too far gone to care.

She really was breathtakingly beautiful. He watched her strip off, her glazed and distant like all the rest, but her body awake with helpless obedience to her secret desire. Underneath the tracksuit she was wearing nothing but a red crop-top and a pair of the purest white cotton panties Alex had ever set eyes on. As she peeled off the top, he saw that her breasts were every bit as perfect as he had imagined: firm, flawless globes exactly the right size to fit into your hand, and tipped with chocolate-coloured nipples that were stiffening into rubbery stalks before his very eyes.

The panties slid down over her athletic hips, revealing a plump mound covered with a short frizz of soft black curls. He breathed in the aroma of her, a piquant scent of cologne and fresh sweat, and wanted more than anything to plunge his dick between those beautiful dark lips.

But he had seen her secret in the glass. And he knew that was not what she wanted.

This is such a waste, he lamented as he unzipped

his pants and released his cock from its prison. Such a terrible waste of this delicious young flesh. He wanted to be deep inside the girl, not doing this. But the box had its rules, and it forced you to play by them. So Alex laid himself down on the dry earth and the girl took things from there, squatting over him so that her feet were on either side of his head and her face was achingly close to his cock.

Her lips touched his glans, kissing him with a kind of innocent wonderment that was hornier than any thousand-pound-a-night whore. His hips bucked as he tried desperately to get her to take him right into her mouth, but he already knew that she wouldn't. He longed to cover her lovely young face with his spunk, spatter her mouth, her eyes, her cheeks, watch his come dripping down her chin, her throat, trickling into the moist valley between her breasts.

Instead of which, he pissed all over her. She groaned with pleasure as he fountained up into her face, drenching her hair, her lips, her breasts. And as she spread her thighs wide and sprayed him with her own golden rain, to his astonishment Alex found himself opening his mouth and drinking it down, as helpless as he had been with Sandi.

It was inexplicable. He hated this kind of thing,

wouldn't have dreamed of doing it in a million years; but here he was, drinking a girl's piss and getting such a buzz out of it that his cock jerked and he came, more powerfully than he could remember doing in a long time. It was almost as though the box delighted in humiliation; in forcing you to take extreme pleasure in the things you found most disgusting.

As luck would have it, Alex didn't have time to ponder on the whys and wherefores. Because at that moment he heard the sound of approaching voices.

And he had a horrible suspicion that the game was up.

Greg was in a bit of a quandary. On the one hand, it wasn't every day that you stumbled across a sensational-looking, totally uninhibited, up-for-anything lay. On the other, she might well be a potentially dangerous psychopath . . .

'Go on,' he said, keeping to his own side of Sylvie's hotel room, though the mini-tyrant in his pants was urging him to get stuck in. 'You'd better tell me the rest.'

'You don't believe me, do you?' said Sylvie accusingly.

There was a desperate look in Sylvie's dark eyes,

and a hint of tears welling up. Oh, bugger, thought Greg. Weeping Frenchwomen: this is all I need.

'Yes I do,' he protested. The look on Sylvie's face remained sceptical. 'Well, all right, maybe I'm not absolutely one hundred per cent certain about all of this, but at least I've got an open mind. That's something, isn't it?'

'I suppose so,' she replied grudgingly.

'Well, then.' He started the tape again. 'You'd better tell me the rest, then I can check it out.'

'You remember,' she began, 'when we were in the park?'

'Er . . . yeees.'

He edged away slightly, still not quite over the embarrassment of seeing Sylvie getting over-friendly with a tree in the middle of Green Park.

'It was happening again,' she said quietly. 'I was having another vision.'

She said it so unaffectedly that Greg couldn't help but at least half believe her.

'What – another sexy one, you mean? Like the one with all the custard and stuff?' he added hopefully.

She nodded glumly. 'But this time I was a man.'

'What – the man you had sex with in the shop? The one you're trying to find?'

124

She shook her head. 'No, I was having sex with him. Only this time I was a man too. And I was wearing a wedding dress.'

Greg edged another six inches along the bed. 'Yeah, right. Well, live and let live, eh?'

'I don't think he realised I was a man, at least, not at first. He seemed quite . . . shocked.'

'You don't say.'

Greg stifled a chuckle, as he imagined how Cindy would react when she heard this tape. Even if it turned out not to be true – which it probably would – it was a bloody good story, and *Mondo Bizarro* had never been that bothered about the truth anyway.

She looked up at him, clearly not finding any of this half as funny as he did. 'This time I heard his name.'

'You did?' Greg pricked up his ears. 'What was it?'

'Alex.'

'Alex what?'

'I don't know.'

'Oh.' Greg's flash of enthusiasm tapered off.

'But surely it is a start, yes?'

'Yeah,' he sighed. 'I guess it's a start.'

He was about to tell her just how many thousand Alexes there must be between Land's End and the

Outer Hebrides, when the faded pop star on the wall-mounted TV screen started introducing the next music video.

'. . . and next up after the break, "Savin' it 4 the 1" from Christian rapper Missy Goody 2Shooz, who was sexually assaulted by a fan in Hyde Park this morning. Police have charged a man, who was taken into custody at . . .'

'Go on,' prompted Greg, not paying the TV much attention. 'You were saying . . .'

'Shh!' Sylvie stared, open-mouthed, at the screen as a flash of news footage showed a young man being led in handcuffs through the door of Lea End Prison. 'That's him!' she exclaimed.

'Who?'

'*Him*.' Sylvie pointed frantically. 'That's Alex!'

8

From the diary of Andreas Hunt

Energy. That was the key. Sexual energy. It had put me in that coffin, and now it was going to get me out.

So at least there was one good thing about being trapped in the cellars of Winterbourne Hall. Winterbourne is, after all, the nation's most happening brothel; and where there's shagging, there's sexual energy – and plenty of it. Mara, clever girl that she is, used her white magic to harness some of that energy – sort of siphon it off, a bit like nicking petrol out of a BMW, not that I had a misspent youth or anything, don't get me wrong.

Well, that didn't actually get me out of there and on my feet again; but it did allow my spirit to escape from time to time, and go walkabout (or should that be floatabout?) round Winterbourne Hall, occasionally finding myself transported into all kinds of people's bodies and even taking part in the odd orgy.

Each time it happened I got a bit better at it; as a matter of fact, you could say I developed quite a talent for manipulation. Like the time I got myself into that guard's body and fucked Mara on the stairs . . . Mmm, I have to say, using some other guy's body to fuck your girlfriend with is a truly unique experience. Hey, don't knock it till you've tried it, OK?

Yeah, I got good at all that manipulation stuff. Maybe I got a little too good at it in the end – you know, got a taste for things you really wouldn't want to have a taste for . . .

'Sir? Mr Weatherall, sir?'

Andreas stopped staring out of the window and broke off his mental rehearsal of the next instalment of his secret diary. He turned round slowly, giving himself time to get back into character.

'What is it now?' he snapped. 'I told you I was not to be disturbed.'

'Yes, sir; sorry, sir.' The young researcher quailed visibly. 'Would you like to beat me now, sir?'

While it was irritating being forced to act the vampire twenty-four hours a day, Andreas had to admit that there were times when he got quite a kick out of inspiring abject terror. He sometimes thought what a blast it would be to go back to the *Daily Comet* – in his new identity – and threaten to do unspeakable things to his old editor. Maybe get one of the Master's gorillas to give him ten inches up the backside and an hour in Heimdal's dungeon . . .

'Just get on with it, Carstairs. I have an appointment with the Master at one.'

'It's about the honeytrap, Mr Weatherall, sir,' explained the young vampire. Secretly, Andreas felt sorry for him; it was less than a month since his initiation (a chance encounter with Anastasia Dubois on the Metropolitan Line) and he was still finding his fangs, so to speak. But Nick Weatherall MP never betrayed the slightest sympathy for anyone but himself.

'Which one?' demanded Andreas wearily. There were so many plots, counter-plots, honeytraps and intrigues going on that he was starting to lose track of it all.

'The plan to entrap the Foreign Secretary, sir.'

'What about it? I thought you were sending Sonja and Natasha to deal with him.'

'Yes, sir; we were, sir.' Carstairs looked distinctly uncomfortable. 'Only . . .'

'Out with it, Carstairs.'

'Only it turns out he doesn't like girls, sir.'

Give me strength, thought Andreas. 'Then find out what he *does* like, imbecile, and act accordingly! What is it – pretty young men? Giraffes?'

Carstairs cleared his throat. 'Domestic appliances, sir.'

The image of the Foreign Secretary dancing through a woodland glade with a fridge freezer passed fleetingly through Andreas's mind. But this was no time to burst out laughing. The one thing guaranteed to get up the Master's nose was failure; and Andreas had no desire to end his days dangling from a meat-hook in Heimdal's cellar.

'Fine. So sort it out. I don't want to know the gory details; just make sure the photos are on my desk by Monday. Or you know what will happen to you, don't you?'

The researcher whimpered softly and disappeared. It was hard to tell if he was terrified or excited; with vampires, it often amounted to the same thing. Andreas leafed through the papers on his desk. Working on a red-top tabloid had stood him in good stead: he was building up quite a file on the caretaker Prime Minister.

All in all, the election campaign was not going too well for Lawrence Manifold. With LeMaitre, the image was consistently squeaky-clean and incorruptible; oh, there might be the odd rumour from time to time, but you could be sure that every one would lead to a dead-end. But as for Manifold . . . incompetent wasn't the word. He had all sorts of rather revolting secrets, which (thanks to Andreas) were starting to come to the surface, like grey scum on cold bathwater.

Andreas did not feel particularly good about helping the Master to almost certain victory. After all, he was the personification of the eternal forces of sensual evil – not to mention a complete bastard. But there was one small consolation; at least the Master had a brain, at least he was competent to rule the world. Lawrence Manifold couldn't even find the end of his own nose without a map.

Sylvie and Greg sat in the car, gazing out at the perimeter wall of the prison. In the darkness it seemed impossibly high, a solid expanse with no break between the blackness of the stones and the blackness of the night sky.

'I told you so,' said Greg, fingers drumming

lightly on the steering wheel. 'Barbed wire, enormous walls, floodlights, security cameras . . . we haven't a cat in hell's chance of breaking in there.'

Sylvie shook her head. She was smiling. 'You don't understand, do you?'

He turned to look at her. 'Understand what?'

'We don't have to break in.' She opened the door and slid out onto the wet cobbles, her thighs creamy in the glow from the streetlamps. 'Just leave this to me, OK?'

'But Sylvie . . .' protested Greg, not exactly in a hurry to put his neck on the line but not that keen on watching her do it for him, either.

'Don't worry, Greg,' she reassured him. Her eyes sparkled. 'There are men in there. Hundreds of men. They'll *welcome* me in.'

She walked unhurriedly across the rainsoaked street. The warm, moist air felt good on her skin and she lifted her face to enjoy the fine mist that was still drifting down out of the dark sky. Her heart was beating frantically, but through excitement, not fear. The drumbeat that Alex had awakened in her sex was beginning to pulse again, forcing her to take chances, to do anything and everything in return for the one thing she craved: sexual pleasure.

This was as good a place as any, she decided. She chose a spot by the main prison gate, right underneath a powerful spotlight, and slid the tortoiseshell combs from her hair, releasing it in dark waves over her shoulders. The street was completely deserted, but she knew that eyes were watching her from inside the prison; hungry eyes that would devour her every move. Well, she would give them something worth looking at.

She needed no music. The drumbeat was already there, inside her, making the walls of her sex pulse and ripple with anticipation. Slowly she began to sway to her own silent music, already tingling with an arousal she knew she could not fight. Her whole body felt as sensitive as the tiny, hot bud between her thighs, which rubbed deliciously against the crotch of her panties with every tiny movement she made.

Watch me, she willed silently as the security camera whirred quietly in her direction. Look at me, desire me. See? I'm doing this just for you. Her fingers slid down over her shoulder, peeling off her jacket with tantalising slowness, revealing a millimetre, and then an inch, and then a whole bare shoulder, decorated with a tiny butterfly tattoo.

The jacket slid to the ground. Underneath, Sylvie

was wearing a tight-fitting black top with thin straps, and a full, floaty skirt whose semi-diaphanous folds revealed the outline of her shapely buttocks and legs. Offering herself to the camera as if it were a lover, she unzipped her skirt and let it creep down her thighs, baring smooth, stocking clad flesh, a tiny white g-string and lace suspenders. She knew she was beautiful, and more sexually arousing than she had ever been in her life before. No man could resist her; nor could she resist him.

The clingy black top peeled from her like a second skin, liberating her bra-less breasts to the warm night air. The mist of fine rain felt delightfully cool on her flesh, puckering her nipples, tautening the two soft globes so that they stood out proud, offering their erect stalks to the lamplight.

She danced there, under the security camera, pouting and coaxing, running her hands over her own breasts, her stocking-clad thighs, the mossy mound beneath her little silky g-string. She knew they would come for her.

And sure enough, she heard keys turn in the locks behind her. And slowly the gate began to swing open.

'Don't stop – whatever you do, don't stop . . .'

The cock was young and eager on Sylvie's tongue. He was hardly more than a boy really, and she knew that she must be careful with him or he would spurt straight away and it would all be over. No, she must make this very special for him; she had a very big favour to ask.

The young prison guard was almost sobbing as she knelt before him on the cold tiled floor of the officers' shower room and took him deep into her mouth. How old was he – eighteen? Not much older, that was for sure. And with his boyish looks he could have passed for several years younger. Sylvie felt like the wicked older woman, leading the virginal boy astray; and the feeling was incredibly erotic.

She tasted the saltiness of his dick and with every droplet her pussy-lips swelled a little more. Moist, sticky-sweet oozings had soaked her panties, and as she knelt before the stranger, sucking hard, she slid her knees a little further apart so that the satin crotch would press harder against her desperately hard clitoris.

It felt good; so good. She couldn't have stopped even if she had tried. Slow and smooth, that was the way; make it last, give him something he would remember her by. Take your time Sylvie, that's right; slip your finger between his arse-cheeks. Feel him shudder and tense as your fingernail begins to tease his puckered hole. Hear him sigh and moan as your finger plunges right inside him. He's loving this, loving this, *loving* this.

When she had held him on the brink so long that she could feel his knees beginning to buckle, she released him at last, making him come in a great explosion of spunk that flooded into her in such abundance that it trickled out of the corners of her mouth, down her chin, over her breasts.

'Lick it up, *chéri*,' she whispered huskily, pulling herself to her feet and drawing his face down to her cleavage. 'That's right, every drop. See how good it tastes.'

As he was lapping at her breasts, Sylvie heard footsteps coming towards them. Her heart skipped a beat as she looked over the guard's shoulder and saw that they were no longer alone.

She shivered with delicious shame as she realised that this was exactly what she had been hoping for.

The handcuffs held her very tightly, chaining her wrists and ankles to the pipes in the shower room, so that she was spreadeagled in a vertical X, completely and utterly helpless to resist.

She had never been more excited in her life.

There were four of them; two young guards,
another in his late twenties and their senior officer,
a powerful man in his forties, muscular and virile,
with a deep scar that ran from the corner of his let
eye to his mouth, giving it a cruel twist. Through
the steam, she saw him unzip his cock and begin to
pump it, hardening it into a fat piston of flesh,
bulbous at his tip and so thick his fingers could
scarcely encircle it.

'Who's been a naughty girl, then?' He grinned
and pinched her cheek.

'Please,' she panted, not sure any more if she
was begging him to stop or go on.

'We're going to have to punish you,' he grinned.
'Sykes, give her the belt, see how she takes to a bit
of discipline.'

One of the younger officers slid his belt out of
its loops and wrapped the end round his hand.

'Give her the buckle end, Jimmy,' said one of
his colleagues. 'Looks like she likes it good and
hard.'

The first blow felt like the stab of a knife as metal
and leather bit into Sylvie's creamy-white buttocks,
raising an angry red welt. Tears sprang to her eyes
but she did not cry out. If she made too much fuss,
they might get frightened and stop. And she knew

now that the one thing she could not bear was for them to stop.

The strokes came thick and fast, expertly administered with a steady rhythm that turned her flesh to fire. At first she was sure she could not bear it, but as she lost count of the blows she began to feel a different sensation invading her body, the pain turning to a kind of erotic heat that pulsed in time to the drumbeat of her sex.

Almost swooning with excitement and exhaustion, she heard the strap fall to the floor, then someone unlocked the cuffs holding her wrists to the pipes. She slipped forward, onto her hands on the wet tiled floor, backside in the air. Something slipped between her buttocks.

'She's good an' wet.'

'Give it her, Wayne. She's beggin' for it.'

Suddenly there was a cock in her mouth, and a cock in her cunt, and another cock forcing its way into the virgin-tight haven of her arse. And the man with the scar was standing and watching, cock in hand, wanking himself to the rhythm of Sylvie's utter degradation.

It felt like paradise.

Semen exploded inside her and she came, her whole body jerking with the sudden ecstasy of her orgasm. It was almost too much to bear. She longed to collapse, to give in, to slide into unconsciousness and rest for a while, but already the need was building up inside her all over again, and there was nothing she could do to fight it.

A tongue forced its way between the lips of her sex, reawakening the hungry little bud, turning it into a tyrant that screamed out for the satisfaction of its owm desires. A cock-burst of spunk filled her mouth, her throat, dripped onto the floor. She gasped and swallowed, drinking down every drop she could with insatiable greed.

'Little slut. You beautiful, filthy-minded little slut.' The man with the scar took a last few, hard strokes and jerked his come onto her face, spattering her eyes, her nose, her cheeks as he grunted with satisfaction.

And Sylvie loved every moment. But still she wanted more.

Alex Carlyle backed away into the corner of his cell, looking distinctly nervous.

'Now hang on a minute . . . what did you say your name was?'

'My name is Sylvie Montana, and I am going to make sure you never forget it!' Sylvie slammed the cell door shut and advanced towards him. 'I hate you, Alex; do you realise how much I hate you?'

He shook his head and tried to look blameless. 'What did I do?'

'Don't give me that, you know damn well what you did.'

'If it's about the desk . . .'

'Screw the bloody desk! Do you realise what you've done to my life, you English bastard?'

Alex licked his lips nervously. 'Er . . .'

'You're pathetic, do you know that? Completely pathetic. And it's all your fault that this is happening to me.'

'I . . . don't . . .'

'Understand? Oh you understand, I know you do. Because you're feeling it too, aren't you?' She stared him straight in the eyes. *'Aren't you?'*

He didn't answer, but she had already glimpsed the fear and lust and recognition in his eyes. She knew she was right; he didn't have to tell her anything.

'This hunger inside me, this terrible hunger that no degradation on earth can satisfy – this is all down to you.'

Alex cut in, trying his best to defend himself. 'Come on, it's not my fault: it's the box.'

She seized on his words. 'So you admit you took the box as well as the desk?'

He looked evasive. 'Look, I'm sorry I nicked your desk, I've sold it on now but I can scrape together a couple of grand if you can get me out of this place . . .'

'Shut up about that bloody desk, and tell me what you've done with the box.'

A horrible silence filled the cell, punctuated only by the distant howling of some deranged inmate. Alex stared down at his prison-issue boots.

'I'm waiting,' said Sylvie.

'I haven't got it.'

'So who has?'

'I don't know. They took it off me when they arrested me.'

'Oh, for goodness' sake! *Who* took it off you?'

'I dunno – the police, I'm not sure.'

She blazed silently at him, wishing she had it in her to punish him the way he deserved to be punished; to make him suffer the way she was suffering now. But maybe he already was, she thought as she looked into his eyes and saw her own terrible hunger reflected there.

'It's the box,' whispered Alex. 'It does this to people; there's nothing you can do to fight it.' He grasped her hand, and she realised that he was shaking. 'There's nothing you can do . . . only give in.'

She wrenched her hand away. 'Don't you dare touch me.'

He fell to his knees on the floor, pawing at her ankles. A low moaning sound came from Alex's parched lips. 'Please, Sylvie. Please let me fuck you. Or suck my dick . . . please, Sylvie, you of all people must understand. I *need* this . . .'

She kicked out at him. 'Lick my foot, slave.'

Pathetically grateful, he grovelled on the floor, covering her feet with wet kisses. 'Mistress. Oh mistress.'

'Not good enough,' she snapped. And grinding his outstretched tongue beneath her heel, she spun round and walked out.

9

I'm in a cage. A tiny cage with black bars. I know
they're black but I can't see them, because there's
something over my eyes and in my throat and round
my neck, and I can't breathe.

There are chains around my wrists and ankles. I
try to pull myself free but the chains are too tight.
And the bars of the cage are moving inward; I can
feel the floor and the walls and the ceiling sliding
in on me, squeezing, compressing, crushing the last
few drops of life out of me. I'm screaming out for
Mara but she can't hear me.

In a moment it will be too late.

Andreas lay flat on his back on the black satin
sheets, staring up at the mirrored ceiling, feeling
the cold sweat trickle into his mouth. A nightmare,
that was all it had been. Just another of those

horrible dreams where he was a helpless prisoner and something terminal was about to happen to him. Recently it had been turning into a nightly ritual. In fact, in his dreams he had died more often than Kenny in 'South Park'.

Mara slept beside him, tendrils of auburn hair snaking over her bare breasts, lips parted, one hand resting on his leg. He decided against waking her. It wasn't as if she could do anything to make the nightmares go away. All he could do was lie here and remind himself that if it wasn't for her, he'd still be stuck inside the crystal.

He thought back to the night she had finally released him from his prison inside the Master's discarded body. There was a massive orgy going on at Winterbourne, something really special to launch the Master's new political career. Andreas's spirit had been well lively by then, straining at the leash to get out, sensing all the erotic energy around it and so desperate to escape that the crystal had cracked around him.

Among the guests that night had been a rookie MP called Weatherall – young, not bad-looking, absolutely loaded – and a total git. If you'd suggested that Nick Weatherall was a tad right-wing, people would have laughed in your face. Even Stalin would have blanched at some of his policies. Added to which, he was as thick as the pigshit on his father's five-thousand-acre farm. Just Andreas's luck that he had ended up inside his body.

Not that he was complaining, quite the reverse. He'd be eternally grateful to Mara and her white magic, luring Weatherall down to the cellars, offering him a quickie on top of the crystal . . . Of course, the Master's plan had been for Mara to initiate Weatherall as a vampire. He wasn't to know that she had a rather different agenda.

One quick shag, a bit of mumbo-jumbo . . . and bingo. Weatherall's spirit and Andreas's had swapped places. It wasn't an ideal solution, but at least the fact that Weatherall was such a waste of space made him feel less guilty about nicking the bloke's body. He wondered how Weatherall was feeling right now, trapped the same way he had been. Bloody awful, probably. Second thoughts, he was so pissed he probably hadn't even noticed yet.

Free at last, thought Andreas, rolling onto his side to escape the shadowy image of Weatherall's face, staring down at him from the mirrored ceiling. That's a bloody laugh. Yeah, he had a body now, and it worked. But that wasn't the end of it, was it? Oh no. He couldn't just up and walk out with Mara, and forget that all of this had happened.

He *was* Nick Weatherall now, or he might as well be. And, since his remarkable intelligence boost, Nick Weatherall just happened to have become one of the Master's favourite underlings, the one who had to be one step behind Anthony LeMaitre whenever there was flesh to be pressed or a keynote speech to deliver.

He slid out the drawer of the bedside table, and took out the dictaphone. Yeah, he was out of the crystal, sure he was. But his new freedom had turned out to be just another kind of prison.

Christian had a vague feeling of unease. Something did not seem quite right about Lea Hall. For one thing, shouldn't a prison have more guards in it?

He dismissed the thought as unimportant. Even if someone was plotting against him, they were doomed to abject failure. For what force on Earth could possibly harm him?

Slipping off his gloves, he slapped them into the Governor's hand.

'Take care of those.'

'Yes, sir; of course, sir.'

An impatient snap of the fingers. 'Chair.'

'Oh, please forgive me, sir, I was forgetting.'

Christian looked on in contempt as the small, balding man in the anonymous grey suit offered him an uncomfortable plastic-seated monstrosity.

'Not *that* one, you cretin.' He shouldered the fumbling imbecile out of his way and helped himself to the Governor's owm chair, pointing to the plastic one. 'You may sit.'

'Sir, I . . .'

'I said *sit*.'

The Governor sat, like a well-trained poodle. 'Yes, sir. Sorry, sir.'

Christian crossed his legs and leaned back in the expensively upholstered swivel chair. 'I hope you are not going to disappoint me. Are you going to disappoint me, Hargrove?'

The small man managed to look nervous and eager, all at once. 'No, sir. I . . . I have it for you sir, just like I said I would.'

The younger man's face relaxed into a cruel smile. 'So. Perhaps you are not quite as pathetic as I had thought. Give it to me.'

The Governor hesitated. 'Sir, I . . .'

'Now, Hargrove. Or do you want me to punish you?'

He scuttled to the door, rattled the handle to ensure that it was locked, then opened his drinks cabinet and reached behind a double row of Highland single malts. 'Here it is, sir.'

The box. Christian's smile grew sly. His fingers had almost closed round it when the Governor hesitated to release his grip on the sparkling trinket.

'Give it to me.'

'Sir,' whined Hargrove. 'You promised me. My reward . . .'

'Ah yes, your reward.' Christian let out a weary sigh. 'Very well, you shall have it. But first, give me the box.' The Governor complied. 'Good dog. Now, as a very special privilege, you may lick my fingers.'

He extended his long, slender hand, and the Governor pressed it to his lips eagerly. 'Oh, thank you, sir, thank you.' Eyes closed, he ran his long pink tongue over the sensitive fingers.

'Enough.' Christian snatched his hand away and picked up his gloves from the desk.

'And the rest of my reward, sir? When shall I have that?'

'Soon,' promised Christian, heading for the door and unlocking it. 'Very soon.'

He stepped out into the empty corridor. Behind him, he heard the sift thud of a body hitting the floor as the Governor clapped his hands to his mouth, convulsed and fell like a stone.

Christian made a mental note to wash the poison from his hands before touching any other mortals – well, ones he wanted to keep, anyway.

Sylvie had been gone a long time, and Greg was getting jumpy. He'd seen her go inside the prison right enough, but since then . . . nothing. He began to imagine all the things that might have gone horribly wrong. This was no good. couldn't just sit here, waiting for something to happen. He had to get out and do something.

Slipping out of the driver's seat, he left the car and started walking round the perimeter wall, hands in pockets. Walking helped him to think. Mind you, thinking gave him no relief, for he kept asking himself how on earth he had allowed himself to get mixed up with this. Covering the Cup Final, that was his bag. Making a bit of extra money on the side, selling tickets to the touts. Not guest-starring in an episode of 'The X-Files'.

The streets were completely deserted. Everybody was at home sound asleep; just like I ought to be, thought Greg gloomily. Then, just as he rounded the corner, he heard the sound of a car engine and instinctively flattened himself against the wall.

The tall black gates of Lea Hall prison dragged open, scraping over the cobbles, and the nose of a shiny black limousine slid slowly out past the lodge. *Hang on a mo*, thought Greg, screwing up his eyes; *I know that numberplate. And who . . . ?*

The car swung out of the prison gates and slid along the road, missing Greg's hiding place by inches. He was so close to the car that he couldn't possibly have been mistaken. The man in the back of the limo was definitely head of the leader of the Opposition's policy unit.

Uh? Greg scratched his head. It didn't make sense. What was a policy bigwig doing in a men's high-security jail? Leisure interests a bit too dodgy for Soho, maybe? Hmm. The old tabloid instincts started to kick in. Now this was interesting. Really interesting.

'Greg? Greg, is that you?'

As he approached the car, he saw her huddled against the bonnet, her crumpled jacket round her shoulders, looking utterly miserable.

'Sylvie? Are you all right?'

She nodded, but she didn't look it. 'I'm fine. But you could have left the car unlocked.'

'Round here? You're kidding. I'm amazed the

hubcaps are still here, as it is.' He unlocked the car and she slid inside. He couldn't help noticing that her hair was hanging in damp rats' tails, and her skin was very pink and moist. There were red marks on her back and legs too, marks that tomorrow would be bruises and weals. 'Sylvie – what on earth happened to you in there?'

'It doesn't matter, OK?'

'Not OK. If you're putting yourself in danger, you're putting me in danger, too – and that's not OK at all. Got that?'

He breathed in the scent of her . . . that unmistakable, musky scent. And he knew exactly what she'd been up to in that prison. The very thought swelled his cock shamefully hard. His imagination was running riot, and he had the most unbearable need to know every voyeuristic detail of what Sylvie had done, who she had bartered her body with, the wonderful, degrading pleasures she had experienced.

'Look, it doesn't matter; none of it matters,' she said irritably, turning her face away. 'I failed.'

'You didn't manage to get to see this Alex guy?'

'Oh, I got to see him. But it was a waste of time: they took it off him when he was arrested in the park. He doesn't have the box any more.'

'Hell.' Greg banged the steering wheel. 'So who does?'

'He says he doesn't know.'

Greg raised an eyebrow. 'And you think he's lying?'

She shook her head. 'No, I'm sure he's telling the truth. And that's not the worst of it.' Sylvie clutched his arm so hard he saw stars. 'I saw it in his eyes, Greg. The box . . . it's doing it to him, too.'

'Doing what? I don't . . .'

'The fire, Greg. The hunger. Burning inside him, eating him up. It's more than he can stand. He wanted me to give him sex, he would have done anything just to lick my shoes, it's that bad, Greg.'

He looked at her, put his hands on her shoulders. 'You're saying . . . it's that bad for you?'

She nodded. 'Terrible. Unbearable. It's there all the time, the need. And if I don't get what I need, the pain . . .' Her voice fell to a hoarse whisper. 'You have to help me, Greg. Please help me.'

At first he didn't see what she was driving at. 'Help you? That's what I'm trying to do, Sylvie. But if we can't get our hands on that damned box of yours . . .'

'Not that way!' The exasperation in her eyes was

turning to fear – and something even deeper and darker. The kind of hunger that went beyond sex, so powerful that Greg couldn't be sure if he was more aroused than he had ever been in his life before, or just scared out of his wits.

Her fingers clawed their way down his back, scratching his flesh through his shirt. 'Don't deny me, Greg, you can't! You have to do this for me, you have to fuck me, don't you see?'

'Sylvie, you're sure you . . . ?'

'Help me, Greg! Help me!'

Fuck a gorgeous French girl in stockings and suspenders? It was the kind of offer no red-blooded male could refuse, not even one sitting in a car outside a maximum security prison, watched by several powerful floodlights and a battery of security cameras. Besides, Sylvie was already taking the initiative, tearing at the buttons on his shirt, ripping it off him with her teeth, fingers scrabbling at his trouser belt.

He decided to help her out. What choice did he have? They both had something the other wanted, and right now the only thing Greg could think about was plunging into that beautiful soft flesh. Thank heavens for reclining seats, he thought as he lay back and let her have her way with him, wrenching

down his pants and kneeling on the passenger seat
beside him, bending over and dangling her full
breasts above him so that the nipples swung to and
fro across the tip of his cock, teasing him with light,
tantalising kisses.

'Wank me,' she pleaded, grabbing his hand and
pushing it between her legs.

He felt the delicious slipperiness of her own
abundant juices, mixed with the cool ooze of other
men's spunk; and, like the pearl at the centre of the
oyster, the small, hard stone of Sylvie's clitoris. It
struck Greg at that moment that this was the best
feeling in the world, having this half-naked beauty
screaming at him to take her to paradise, and
practically begging him to give it her any which
way he wanted. Kind of scary, too, but maybe that
just made it better.

His fingertip began to circle the French girl's
pleasure centre, teasing her, giving her just enough
to drive her through the ceiling of wanting. She was
pushing herself down onto his hand now, almost
fucking herself with hard, jerky movements of her
hips that made her breasts jiggle against his
throbbing glans.

'Don't you dare stop,' he gasped, praying he
could keep her on the edge for about a hundred

years. 'Whatever you do, don't . . .'

She did stop. But only to slide across onto his seat, and position herself over the vertical spike of his dick. Her own hands held her sex wide apart, and a flood of pearly juices escaped from between her swollen lips as she drove down on him, forcing him high up into her sex, swallowing him up in the adorable maw of her pussy.

Breasts bouncing and slapping against his upturned face, Greg lay back and let Sylvie have her wicked way with him. It was like being eaten alive and it was fantastic. Somewhere at the back of his mind, he had the slight feeling that he ought not to be taking advantage of this poor girl's obvious mental instability; but then again, what true-born Englishman would turn down a damsel in distress?

The next morning, Greg arrived at work feeling distinctly hung-over. Whether it was the lack of sleep, or the after-effects of being ravished in the front seat of a Clio, it was difficult to say. All he knew for sure was that what had happened the night before had happened without him making any conscious decision. The fact was, he couldn't have turned down Sylvie Montana if she'd been a hundred and fifty-two – and that was just her waist measurement.

Something very peculiar was going on around here.

He spent the day on automatic pilot, trying not to yawn too obviously in the editorial meeting and sketching out his strategy on the back of an empty doughnut box. He would have sloped off home early, only Cindy hadn't shown up all day and he desperately needed to talk to her.

Around half-past six, when he'd all but given up hope, she swanned in looking like Liz Hurley meets Cruella de Vil, in a red and black sequined outfit that was so thin it clung to her like a second skin, and couldn't have weighed more than a couple of ounces even if you threw in the red silk thong.

'Blimey,' said Fat Roland, taking a sneaky peek down her sequined cleavage. 'Don't get many of them to the pound.'

'You should know,' replied Cindy sweetly, grabbing Roland's chest through his sweaty polo shirt. 'Hmm, forty-six B, time you bought yourself a new bra. What is it, Greg?' she demanded, wheeling round to confront him as he cleared his throat for the umpteenth time.

'I just wanted a quick word.'

'Go on, then.' She flashed a humourless smile. 'There, that's three already.'

'In private.'

'It'll have to wait till tomorrow.' She flicked her fur stole over her shoulder and rattled away on her computer keyboard. 'Can't be late, I'm due at the media awards dinner. Just popped in to check my e-mails.'

'Cindy,' insisted Greg, interposing himself between her and the screen.

'Shove off, Greg, you're getting on my tits.'

And what great tits they were, mused Greg, wondering how anything that size managed to stay so perky without the aid of scaffolding. 'Cindy please, just five minutes. It's urgent.'

There must have been something convincing in his tone of voice, because she left off clicking her mouse and glanced up. 'Urgent as in life or death, or urgent as in, you've got a quid stuck in the condom machine again?'

'Cindy, be serious. You know I wouldn't ask if it wasn't important.'

'She straightened up. 'Hmm. This had better be good, Greg, or your immortal soul is mine. Come on, then.'

He trailed her out of the office. 'Come on where?'

Cindy stepped into the lift. 'You've got the length of time it takes me to hail a taxi. Better get on with it.'

The lift descended irritatingly quickly. 'I think I'm on to a political.'

'Oh yes?' Cindy's voice betrayed interest. 'Details?'

'Can't tell you right now. But it's going to be a big one, and I've got a grade-A lead.'

The lift stopped at the ground floor and Cindy strode out past the reception desk to the big glass doors. 'How much is this going to cost me, Greg?'

'Nothing.'

'Oh yeah, ha ha. I wasn't born yesterday. Taxi!'

He followed her out onto the pavement. 'I'm serious. It won't cost you anything.'

'So where's the catch?'

'There isn't one. I just need the contact number for that Malabari fortune teller who wrote volume three of the "Kama Sutra".'

'Oh you do, do you?' Cindy cursed under her breath as a black cab sped right past her and disappeared into the rush-hour traffic. She cast Greg an amused look. 'What for – going off me already?'

'I need it for . . . leverage,' he replied. He knew it sounded over-mysterious, but at this stage he didn't feel he could go into detail. Keep things close to your chest till you know it's in the bag, that's what his first editor had advised him, and it was bloody good advice.

Another two taxis sailed past. 'Oh hell, I'm going to have to walk. And these shoes are killing me.'

Greg followed her as she set off along the road, turning off to take a short cut down a side-street behind an old warehouse, and fell in step beside her. 'Cindy, how could anybody go off you?'

She laughed. 'Trying to make up to me so you can get what you want?'

'What I want right now is you.'

'Now hold on . . .'

'I mean it.' He caught her arm and pressed her back against the wall of a derelict shop. He wasn't spinning her a line; at that moment, at least, he meant every word he was saying. Slowly he slipped down her left strap and kissed her bare shoulder, then did the same with the right.

'Greg . . . this dress . . .'

He pulled gently on the superfine fabric, and the bodice of the dress flipped down to her waist, revealing Cindy's remarkably fine breasts. 'God Cindy, why do you hide these away? They're incredible.'

His teeth nipped the sensitive flesh and she squirmed, no longer the ice maiden she liked to play in the office, but completely at the mercy of her own sensual needs. 'Greg, you *bastard*.'

Taking that as a compliment, he held her breast firm and suckled it as his other hand crept down over her thigh and began ruching up her skirt. It whispered softly against the distant hum of traffic as he pushed it up over her red silk thong, stretched tight over her hard, plump mound.

Not even bothering to pull down her panties, he simply pushed aside the gusset and hoisted her up onto his dick, her legs round his waist, one high-heeled shoe dangling from her toe as he humped her hard against the rough brick wall.

Afterwards, as she lay across his shoulder, she whispered in his ear, 'OK, you win.'

'Win what?' he asked innocently.

'Don't give me that, you know what. That contact number, you can have it.'

'Thanks.'

'You're a manipulative bastard, you do know that?'

'Oh, definitely.'

She kissed him on the end of the nose and jumped down, retrieving her fallen shoe.

'Just be careful, OK? Now, get me a taxi in the next two minutes, or you're dead meat.'

10

'The thing is,' mused Andreas to his dictaphone, 'it wouldn't be so bad if I could see an end to it. But here the two of us are, forced to play permanent supporting roles in the Master's theatre of the absurd. It's like doing permanent rep in Scunthorpe, only worse; because if you get bad reviews here, you stand to lose more than your Equity card.

'Ever since we found ourselves in these bodies, Mara and I have had to use talismans to protect ourselves from the Master's psychic power. Just as well Mara knows her way round a grimoire. Otherwise he'd see through the deception straight off – and as it is, we've had a few narrow squeaks. And so life goes on . . .'

'Only it isn't life, is it?' pointed out Mara. 'Not real life, anyhow.'

'To tell you the truth, I think I've lost track of

what real life is,' confessed Andreas, with a sudden yearning to be sitting in The Dog & Duck with his mates from the *Comet*, eating pork scratchings and wondering how he was going to pay the rent. 'Everything's been completely weird ever since . . .'

Mara laid a hand on his shoulder. 'Ever since you met me?'

He undid the top button of her flimsy white skirt and planted a trail of kisses that led all the way from her throat to the bottom of the valley between her breasts. 'If it wasn't for you, I'd have gone *completely* crazy by now.'

His fingers fumbled with the next button, but Mara wriggled out of his grasp. 'Aren't you supposed to be summarising those opinion poll results for the Master?'

Andreas felt his stomach drop to his boots. His gaze drifted to the pile of papers on his desk. Weird? he thought, don't talk to me about weird. In all the time he'd been the Master's chief political dogsbody, he'd never known anything as weird as this. In just two days, Anthony LeMaitre's approval rating had dropped nearly ten per cent.

'I am in sooo much shit,' he confided.

'Maybe the market research people have made a mistake . . .'

He shook his head. 'There's no mistake, Mara. Even a gerbil could tell those figures add up to bad news.' He swallowed, trying not to think about how that news was going to go down with the Master.

He didn't know how, and he couldn't begin to guess why; but something, very definitely, had changed.

The Great Hall had been transformed into the innermost circle of Hell.

The walls dripped with streaks and swirls of red and black paint, iridescent in the flames that danced on the waters of the sunken pool. Luridly painted bodies coupled on the mosaic floor, rolling over and over in the cool, slippery mess of spunk and sweat and blood. A naked girl hung from the domed ceiling in silver chains, over a pit seething with sex-hungry vampires, reaching and clawing for her fresh virgin flesh as she was lowered, inch by inch, towards her inevitable fate.

It was undoubtedly one of Winterbourne's finest orgies. Heimdal, Lord of Winterbourne, had excelled himself this time, creating the perfect environment in which to nurture his Master's lustful rage.

Sedet, the Master's immortal queen, was doing

her utmost to drive him into a frenzy of jealous hunger. She was dressed as Queen of the Damned, in a tight-fitting robe of fine black leather, slashed to the waist. Lazing on a red velvet chaise longue, she was enjoying the attentions of three masked demons, the panels of her skirt falling open about her thighs, revealing the enormous diamonds which studded her shaven sex-lips.

These three youths had been kidnapped from a remote Italian seminary, and Sedet had taken very special pleasure in corrupting their fragile innocence. Under her strict tutelage, they had quickly become adept at all the skills of sensual depravity. As the youngest of the demons bowed his head between her thighs, lapping at his mistress's cunt with his silver-sheathed tongue, Sedet brought her whip down upon his back, drawing a thin, beaded line of blood and making him squirm with delight. His companions fawned about their queen like wolf-cubs, each taking one pierced dug between their lips and drinking the delicious venom from her breasts.

It was a display calculated to whet the Master's appetite, for he liked nothing better than to take his pleasure while he observed his queen's command of her slaves. But, although the slave-boy offered up his pretty backside with whimpers of longing, the Master pushed him aside with an impatient sweep of his arm.

'Your report,' he rapped out, looking from one twin to the other, his eyes fathomless grey steel.

The male twin licked his lips, his eyes flicking towards the sticky tangle of coupling bodies. 'Master, might we be permitted . . . ?'

'You may not.' The grey eyes glittered. The smile was thin-lipped and cruel. 'You may look, but you may not touch.'

The female twin let out a soft, tormented sigh. 'Oh, Master,' she pleaded, kneeling beside the Master's throne and stroking his sleeve. 'Your Highness, my royal lord . . .'

'You are my slaves, and you will control your appetites.' The Master's teeth glittered sharply in the dancing flames. 'Or I shall control them for you. Now. Give me your report before I lose my patience.'

The twins exchanged looks. He was playing with them, that much was obvious, and that could mean only one thing. He *knew*.

'Master,' began the male twin. 'We have done as you . . .'

'. . . instructed,' went on his sister. 'We have kept a close watch . . .'

'. . . on the Frenchwoman . . .'

'And the box?' enquired the Master, with menacing precision. Clicking his fingers, he summoned a crystal dagger out of thin air and used its razor-sharp point to pare his fingernails.

There was a short and horrible silence. Behind the twins, two damned souls shrieked with glee as they fucked in the heart of the flames, ripping each other's flesh as they coupled, knowing that however much pain they inflicted would all be healed; for they were the Master's faithful disciples, the glorious legion of the undead.

'We . . . do not have it,' confessed the girl.

'It has . . . disappeared.'

The Master's fingers tightened around the blade of the crystal dagger, his knuckles whitening with anger.

'So, you have failed me.'

'Master . . .'

'Again. And now I must punish you.' The Master frowned. This was a great inconvenience and he was in a particularly foul humour tonight, grand orgy or not. Pain? Oh yes, he could inflict any amount of pain upon the two of them, but they would only thank him and beg him for more. Degradation? Base humiliation? They would weep with gratitude as he crushed their faces into the dirt.

No. There was only one fitting punishment for this pair of errant slaves.

The Master fixed his gaze upon the male twin. 'Approach.'

Reluctantly, the twin climbed the steps to the throne. 'Master, we wish only to serve you. We will not fail you again.'

'Indeed you will not.'

Eager to do its Master's bidding, far more obedient than any slave, the crystal dagger obeyed his thought and flew through the air, neatly severing the twin's right index finger at the knuckle.

'Master . . . !' cried the she-twin, rushing to her brother's aid.

He stared at his mutilated hand in astonishment. Blood spurted from the stump, splashing onto the white tiles at the base of the throne, then evaporated without trace, as though it had never been. But, inexplicably, the hand did not repair itself.

'Master . . . !' he exclaimed. 'Master, what have you done to me?'

'This time,' replied the Master with malice, 'it will not grow back. I have that power. In fact, I have many powers; you would do well to remember that.'

The girl twin's eyes filled with tears. 'But Master
. . . Master, we are no longer true twins!'

'Get out of my sight,' replied the Master,
dismissing them like a game that had lost all interest.
'And have Heimdal send me three of the new
initiates. I feel curiously hungry tonight.'

Alex was feeling distinctly sorry for himself.

Ever since that peculiar night, when Sylvie had
visited him and the prison governor had died in
mysterious circumstances, he had had the strange
feeling that he was being victimised. And, not to
put too fine a point on it – he was.

As if that wasn't bad enough, he had been woken
up at five o'clock in the morning, given a plastic
bag to cram his stuff into, and bundled into the back
of an armoured van without so much as a blanket
over his head to maintain his dignity. Mind you,
there wasn't much of that left, and it wasn't as if
anybody gave a toss about him anyway.

He'd been sitting all alone in the back of the van
for ages now, and nobody had even bothered telling
him where he was going. For all he knew, he was
about to be conveniently disposed of down some
old mine-shaft. What else could you do with an
embarrassing remand prisoner who spent all day

begging everyone from the chief warder to the chaplain for sex?

It was agony. Nobody understood; how could they? Even he could hardly get his head round the idea of a box that made people horny. And not just a bit horny, either. So painfully, desperately, agonisingly sexed-up that there was no escape from it, even in your dreams.

He felt the low fire in his belly beginning to kindle into something hotter, something that screamed to be satisfied. And helplessly he closed his eyes and began to rub himself against the inside of the van, pushing his hardening dick against the hard mesh grille that separated his cage from the driver's compartment. But it was no use, there was no relief. There was nothing but the terrible, aching need, and the slow trickle of clear fluid oozing from his cock-tip, soaking his pants.

Suddenly, the van jerked to a halt, its wheels crunching on something that sounded like gravel or dried-out old branches. For a long time, nothing happened. Then Alex heard keys jangling, and the back door of the van swung open, letting in a flood of cold white moonlight.

He blinked. There was a figure silhouetted against the sky, a tall young woman in a shiny black leather catsuit and spike-heeled thighboots; a black-haired goddess with crimson lipstick and eyes that glittered in the pale oval of her face.

Her breasts were full and soft. He moaned with need as her gloved hand tugged at the zipper on her catsuit and it slid down a few tantalising inches, exposing their creamy muzzles, nuzzling against the leather.

'Help me,' he gasped. 'I don't know who you are, but you've got to help me . . .' His body jerked against the grille, his swollen dick straining to reach her, his fingers clutching at the unyielding mesh.

'Oh, but you're so wrong,' she purred, in a voice that sounded like double cream. 'I don't have to do anything I don't want to, don't you know that?'

He looked into her beautiful, despicable face, and saw that she was laughing at him; but he had lost all self-esteem so long ago that he didn't even care. All that mattered was persuading her to answer the need in him.

'Please . . .' he begged.

'Call me "Mistress".'

He would have said anything, done anything, to get what he needed. 'Please, *Mistress*.'

'Good dog.' She unlocked the grille and

beckoned to him. 'Come closer, dog. That's right, on your knees.'

He crawled to the back door of the van and expected her to get him to jump down, but she halted him at the last moment. 'Stay where you are.' Her cool, slim, leather-sheathed fingers found the zipper on his prison-issue jeans and slid it down with clinical efficiency. 'Now, do not move a muscle or make a sound, or I shall stop. Do you hear?'

Alex nodded, tears pricking the undersides of his eyelids as he screwed his eyes up tight and forced himself to be quiet, when all he wanted to do was cry out loud.

A gloved hand encircled Alex's dick, and began to pump him rhythmically, with a machine-like accuracy of touch that made him feel at once completely humiliated and unbelievably aroused. It was like being wanked by a beautiful android, and he began to imagine that the leather glove concealed fingers of pure steel, so strong and cruel that at the slightest sign of disobedience they would crush his hypersensitive flesh till he screamed for mercy.

His teeth were clenched, his lips tight shut, his breath coming in shallow, rapid gasps. He felt his orgasm rolling up on him like a huge tidal wave, rising up, foamy and white, towering above him, threatening to crash down and destroy him at any moment.

I must not make a sound. I must not cry out, I must not move, or she will punish me. The beautiful robot woman will destroy me . . .

It was weakness, not bravado, that made him shudder and cry out, falling forward onto his hands as he spurted his ecstasy.

She stood and watched him, a mocking smile on her face. 'Bad dog.'

'Forgive me.' He looked up at her, still panting, his dick still hard and already beginning to throb again. 'Forgive me, mistress.'

She snapped her fingers. 'Come, dog. Come with me.'

He jumped down from the van and saw that it was parked in the middle of nowhere, amid a dense copse on the edge of a road he didn't recognise.

'Where are we? Where are you taking me?'

She did not answer, just turned and led the way. And he followed in her wake, secretly suspecting that if she had commanded him to follow her into the mouth of Hell, he would have done so. Without question.

* * *

Sylvie was dreaming of tropical sun, and wonderful, warm beaches.

She was lying on her back on hot, white sand, at the very edge of the ocean. It felt so good, so unbelievably good. As she lay there, so lazy and too drunk with pleasure to move, she felt the sea's warm waves begin to lap at the fringes of her sex. Slowly yet greedily, she spread her legs wide to the foam and let it tumble over her, into her, its little insistent eddies making lazy love to her eager clitoris.

Mmm, good. So good. Sylvie's hands crept up from the sand, over her body, seeking out her own breasts. Above her, the sun burned scarlet through her closed eyelids, the colour of passion. She began to fondle herself, pinching and stroking her nipples, loving herself in ways that only she could, for no other lover could ever know her body so well. And yet it was as if she were discovering it for the first time, awakening new sensations, exploring new aspects of her own sensual beauty as her fingers walked down over her belly, stroked her flanks and backside.

There was a voice. A soft voice, very warm and attractive. Where it was coming from, or who it belonged to, she had no idea. But she liked it. And it was calling to her to masturbate. How strange, that it should be urging her to do the very thing she wanted to do more than anything else. Perhaps it was the voice of her own subconscious desire.

It really was quite odd. Her hands felt like a stranger's hands, and yet they knew her body so well that they could only be her own. Her left hand lingered on her breast, the right slipping between her thighs, sending her index finger smoothly into the tight haven of her arse while her thumb began to rub the already swollen stalk of her clitoris.

Moving her hips seemed the natural thing to do, and she began to flex gently on the hot sand, pushing herself up to meet the luxurious downthrust of her own thumb and forefinger, while with her left hand she pinched and squeezed and teased her nipple into a tingling bud of sensation.

She would have loved it to last for ever, but it was too intense. The climax came with such a rush of delicious energy that it woke her, and she found herself lying panting on her own bed.

At first she did not recognise her own bedroom. It seemed to be filled with a sweet-smelling, luminous mist; and there was a figure standing at the very centre of it. She couldn't make out who it was, but knew it was the owner of the voice. And whoever that was, she needed him, her, it, so much that she would have done anything to keep it with her always.

So much that, at its very first touch, she melted into absolute obedience.

It was inconveniently late by the time Greg had done everything he needed to do.

His first thought was to go straight back to his own flat, get a few hours' shut-eye and then go round to see Sylvie in the morning. What he had to tell her would keep till then, and he was still faintly embarrassed by the things he and Cindy had been up to. Somehow it didn't seem quite fair to take advantage of Sylvie's helpless erotomania, only to sneak off round the corner for a quick knee-trembler with his boss. Besides, a man only had just so much lead in his pencil; and Sylvie's sexual demands were starting to take their toll.

Then he thought of poor Sylvie, all alone in that featureless hotel room, not to mention the bottle of wine that would be sitting on ice and the French girl's irresistibly feminine curves, and he thought, *what the heck. I can always phone in sick.*

The lift took an age to get up to the fifth floor. Was he imagining it, or was his hair starting to thin on top? They really shouldn't put mirrors in lifts; they made people neurotic.

The door of number 515 was standing slightly ajar, and he could see the soft glow from the bedside lamp through the chink in the door.

'Sylvie?' he called out, slipping off his jacket and stepping inside. 'Sylvie, it's me. I'm back.'

But the bed was empty, the window was standing open. And there was not a trace of Sylvie Montana.

11

From the diary of Andreas Hunt

He found out, of course. Well, it was bloody
inevitable really, wasn't it?

There he is on live TV, being grilled about
his policies by this hard-faced blonde, and he
thinks he's really softening her up, doesn't
he? Getting ready to wipe the floor with her
and her Gestapo-style interviewing technique.
Then, just when he thinks he's got her eating
out of his hand, wetting her pants for a chance to
kiss his arse, Little Miss Ice-Maiden goes for the
throat.

'So, Mr LeMaitre, you don't find the recent poll
results a little . . . ah . . . disturbing?'

The smile freezes on his face. 'Poll results?
Whatever do you mean? The poll results have all

been excellent, Genevieve. In fact, we have every expectation . . .'

Her carefully-tweezered eyebrows arched spitefully. 'Excellent, Mr LeMaitre?'

'Certainly.'

She laughed right into Camera number three. 'Well, I realise you're anxious to put a brave face on things, but surely not even your spin doctors can turn a fall of eleven per cent in your personal approval rating into a dazzling tour-de-force . . .'

Well, the Master didn't need to say anything, did he? Not one word. For once, he'd really been caught with his pants down. I mean, you could tell from the look on the his face he hadn't a bloody clue. And why hadn't he? Because I'd been sitting on the poll results, that's why. All right, so it wasn't the brightest of things to do. Sooner or later he was bound to find out the truth, but I guess I was hoping another poll would come in and show him thirty percentage points up. No such luck.

Anyhow, he covers up pretty well while Genevieve Harman's got him in front of the cameras; but by the time he comes off air I'm downing double whiskies in the Green Room, practically incontinent with terror. I'm still wearing the magical talisman, of course, the one Mara made for me, with the ju-ju power topped right up to the limit. But this time I'm sure my luck's going to run out. This time, the bastard who nicked my body is going to see right through this pathetic disguise ad twig who I really am . . .

'You imbecile!' The door rattles in its frame as he slams it behind him. Oh, God, it's worse than I thought. His eyes are glowing dark red – I kid you not, just like in a low-budget horror flick – and he's bawling me out so loud I swear half of London can hear him. 'Try to deceive me, would you? *Would you?*'

I open my mouth and just kind of stand there, pretty sure that whatever I say next is just going to make things worse. I have that talent. Then the door opens and she walks in. Genevieve Harman. And she's laughing all over her face.

'Oh dear, oh dear,' she purrs, taking one look at the Master's hands, six inches from my throat. 'Don't tell me your campaign manager forgot to tell you about the poll results? That was very careless of him . . .'

And that's about all she has time for in the way of gloating, because the Master's on to her like a leopard on a gazelle. She screams as he throws her up against the wall, but no sound comes out. He has her mesmerised. The only sound is the hoarse rasp of her breathing, and the soft tearing sound as he seizes a handful of her blouse and rips it down.

'Master,' I manage to blurt out, thinking of the field day the TV station's going to have if some researcher swans in here and finds the leader of the Opposition ravishing its top political interviewer over the vol au vents. 'Master, don't you think ... ?'

'Silence!' he hisses. The woman's body is trembling, she's shaking her head, trying to tell him to stop, but he's tearing off her bra, lifting up her skirt and ripping it from her belly and thighs like strips of fresh red flesh.

The rest? You can guess it; you don't need me to draw a map for you. It wasn't so much sex as a quick between-meals snack. And don't bother feeling too sorry for Genevieve Harman, because when it came down to it, she was just as peckish as he was. Her lips were saying no, but her body was saying yes, if you know what I mean.

He had her across the table, sending trays of wine-glasses crashing to the floor. Shards of broken glass were sticking right into her flesh, but she didn't even notice. She was under his spell, her eyes were locked into his gaze; she wasn't even trying to protest any more. In fact, her semi-naked body arched to meet his cock as it plunged between her thighs, and then she started clawing at his back, begging him to fuck her harder.

Which, naturally, he did. It was an efficient performance, savage and swift (ten out of ten for technical merit, two for artistic interpretation). At the moment of climax, I saw the Master's teeth fasten on the girl's throat. Forgive me if I don't sound too shocked, only I'd seen it all before. A little sigh, a little blood, and Genevieve Harman was no more than an empty carcass, lying crumpled about his feet.

I'll never forget the way the Master looked at me as he stepped over her still-warm body. The pure menace in his eyes as he glared through me, so hard I thought I was going to burst into flames.

'*That* is how we deal with problems, Weatherall. Now, get this place cleaned up. There is important work to be done.'

Christian watched the box. It watched him back, its rudimentary self-awareness cowed by his superior will.

He smiled at its pathetic attempts to test his power. 'I've heard so much about you, little box. So many secrets.'

Picking it up as though it were a favourite pet, he walked up the final flight of stairs which led to the attic room. It was an old house, solidly built with walls of Cotswold stone that made it easy to keep secrets inside. Three storeys of beamed ceilings were topped off by one huge attic room, built right under the eaves.

Christian was particularly fond of this part of the house, his playroom. It was roasting hot in summer, ice-cold in winter, exactly how he liked it. In fact, he had had the room specially constructed with his pleasure in mind, a cloud-palace high in the sky, with large skylights that let in sights and sounds of the outside world without letting anything out. Least of all his victims. A series of complicated locks on the door made doubly certain that none of his pleasures risked exposure to prying eyes. He locked the door carefully behind him, musing on how disappointingly easy it had been so far.

There were four other people in the room; or more accurately, there were two who were human and two who were not. The vampire sluts sprang forward the moment Christian walked in. They were hungry, and greeted their master's return like half-starved she-cats, fawning on him, pawing at his clothes, offering him their bodies for his pleasure.

'We have done as you commanded, Master,' purred the slut in tight black leather, unzipping her breasts and rubbing them against Christian's chest.

Not to be outdone, Taz – naked save for her crystal slave-collar – offered him a gold-handled whip. 'Flay me, Master,' she pleaded. 'Will you not flay me? I have been a good girl . . .'

Few could have resisted such tempting flesh, but Christian pushed them roughly aside and walked forward, his gaze fixed on his coveted prize.

'So,' he smiled thinly. 'I have you at last.'

Alex and Sylvie lay spreadeagled before him, naked on wooden benches, their bodies held fast with iron bands and leather straps.

'You!' hissed Sylvie, her wrists straining against their iron manacles. 'You have done this to me!'

'Indeed I have, *ma chérie*.' The smile grew ironic. He drew a sharp fingernail abruptly down her belly, raising beads of dark-red blood. 'How interesting. See, my sluts. See how her nipples harden; this one could easily be schooled to the discipline of pain.'

'Let me!'

'No, let me, Master!'

The sluts clamoured to be allowed to do their slavemaster's work. 'See,' cried the leather-princess triumphantly, snapping silver nipple-clamps into place on her victim's body. 'See how she loves her mistress's touch.'

'You are not her mistress!' snapped Taz, twisting strands of Sylvie's hair about her fingers and watching her face contort in pain. 'See how she answers to *my* touch.'

'*Your* touch!' sneered her companion, curling her hand into a fist that turned her row of heavy crystal rings into jagged teeth. 'Your touch is nothing. Only I have the skill to corrupt her to our master's will.'

'You bastard!' Sylvie writhed and twisted, but there was no escape. The curled fist rammed hard between her thighs, forcing its way inside her with such searing pain that she screamed out loud. But there was something worse than the pain, and that was the pleasure; the terrible, treacherous warmth that flooded through her martyred body as the fist twisted inside her, tormenting her, taunting her with the knowledge of her own corruptibility.

'Enough,' commanded Christian. The vamps hesitated. 'I said, *enough*!' They sprang away, cowering and panting, their eyes still fixed on the quivering body of their prey.

'No,' moaned Sylvie, desperately trying to pull her thighs together so that she could squeeze her pussy-lips against each other and find some way of giving herself relief. 'No, you can't leave me like this.'

'Can't I?' He held up the box, moving it teasingly in the sunshine that flooded in through the skylight, making very sure that both Sylvie and Alex got a very good look at the wicked little trinket. 'I'm afraid you're wrong, Sylvie. I can do anything I choose.'

The box glittered maliciously. 'You see this? You remember what it can do?' He saw from their eyes that they remembered, and that even though Sylvie had never seen the box before, she recognised it instantly as the author of all her woes. 'Of course you do, how could you forget? This is the power-giver, the betrayer of dark fantasies, it brings ecstasy . . . or eternal torment.

'Which is it to be, I wonder?'

Stooping, he positioned the mirrored box on the polished wooden floor, between the two punishment tables.

'You may release them.'

The sluts stared at him. 'But . . . Master?'

'Release them. Now.'

The sluts complied, unlocking the iron bands and unbuckling the straps which held Alex and Sylvie captive. Whether she understood more quickly than Alex what she needed to do, or whether she was simply a fraction more agile, Sylvie never knew. All she could be certain of was that she reached the box first, snatching it away just as Alex threw himself forward to grab it.

As she held up the spy-glass it clouded, then cleared, releasing the full force of Alex's fantasy. Suddenly, mechanically, she found herself picking up the gold-handled whip that Taz had discarded. There was no choice, no conscious volition in the action. It was as if some vengeful, lascivious force had taken her over and was using her body to carry out its own perverted desires.

'Worm,' she hissed.

Alex fell to his knees before her, shaking. 'Mistress.'

The whip thrashed across his shoulders and she saw his cock stiffen, jerking suddenly upward. 'Miserable, unworthy creature.'

'Punish me,' he breathed. 'Beat me, humiliate me, defile me, Mistress. I am unworthy.'

Sweat began to drip down Sylvie's body, pooling at the base of her spine, in her navel, between her breasts. She felt the power of sexual frenzy thicken and grow around her as she forced the whip-handle deep into Alex's arse, filling his deepest, darkest desire.

Energy waves were radiating from Alex's body. Waves of wonderful, life-giving sexual power. The sluts watched on in barely-disguised lust, rubbing and pinching their own flesh as they pleaded with their master to give them what they craved. At last he grew weary of their childish squabbling.

'Very well, slaves. You may feed.'

The two vampire sluts fell upon Alex, attaching their hungry nakedness to his body, sucking out every last drop of his sexual energy. Only then, when all was as he wished it to be, did Christian submit to his own hunger.

And engulfed Sylvie Montana in his lust.

Greg had been making enquiries in his usual manner – posing as a Water Board official in search of a leak. It wasn't very original, but it had produced excellent results over the years; besides which, at least one in eight housewives was guaranteed to be sufficiently randy and bored to be up for a quick one over the tumble-dryer.

Greg sat in the trendy bar of the Hotel Transcontinental, drinking tequila and considering his options. Unfortunately nobody had seen anything, or at least if they had, they weren't admitting to it. On the other hand, he had got laid twice, so it wasn't all bad news. The question was, what next?

What next turned out to be a lissome brunette in Dolce & Gabbana combat pants and the kind of tiny designer vest-top that made you think of two ripe melons in a string bag.

'Hi. You can buy me a drink if you like.'

Strewth, thought Greg. What is this – national seduce-a-journo day? She slid onto the bar-stool next to his, filling his nostrils with the scent of Calvin Klein cologne. He noticed that her features were delicate, almost elfin beneath her chic brown crop, but her lips had an almost Latin fullness that set his fantasies racing. Lips just made for giving a man the blow-job of a lifetime.

'What would you like?'

Her smile was wicked, knowing. 'Are we still talking about drinks?'

Her breast rubbed against his arm as she leaned over to help herself to a cashew nut. He handed her the bowl. 'Whatever.'

She ordered a chilled beer, and rolled the bottle over her bare arms, cooling the overheated flesh. 'It's hot in here.'

He loosened his shirt collar. 'You can say that again.'

Eyes the colour of sea-mist fixed his gaze. 'Are you the man who's been looking for Sylvie Montana?'

Greg almost choked on his tequila. 'I might be. Why?'

'I met her. In fact, she screwed me. Want to know more?'

It was the kind of question that really didn't beg and answer, and the girl didn't wait for one. 'I was on an Inter-City,' she said, sipping her beer. 'Me and my boyfriend, we were travelling up from the Cotswolds to London. This French girl . . . the train was half-empty, but she came and sat opposite us. At first I thought she was hitting on Steve – that's my bloke – but then I felt her playing footsie with me under the table, and I think, hello . . .

'Now don't get me wrong, I'm not narrow-minded. If a girl wants to fuck a girl, that's fine. Just don't count me in, OK? It's not my bag. Only that day, it was different.'

Greg tipped the rest of his drink down his throat. He was starting to feel distinctly warm. 'You mean, you and she . . . ?'

'Oh, yeah; I wanted it, see. Wanted her. I mean,

to be honest, Steve could have been abducted by aliens and I wouldn't have noticed. I stopped noticing he was even there. And all the time this French girl's getting more and moire upfront, she's not even trying to hide it. She's leaning over the table, stroking my tits, telling me how pretty they are and how I ought to show them off more. People are staring but it's like she couldn't care less, and neither could I.

'"Come on," she says. "Come with me." I don't bother asking where, I just get up and walk off, leaving Steve staring at me. We go into the toilet together, and we can't keep our hands off each other. Two whole hours we were in there. She gets me to take off my knickers and sits me on the washbasin. I've never been licked out by a girl before – hell, it was good. That tongue . . . If I close my eyes I can still feel it on my clit. And all the time I've got my hands down her bra, squeezing her tits . . .'

She took a swig of beer, licking the wetness from her lips.

'And then?' asked Greg.

'And then she got me to do the same to her.' The girl looked him up and down and he knew – or perhaps he just hoped – what she was going to say next. 'I could do it to you, if you like.'

'You . . . ?'

Her hand sneaked onto his lap and homed in on the agonising swelling in his trousers. 'You're beautifully hard, and I'm beautifully wet. We both have something the other one needs. So how about it?'

Which was how Greg found himself in the Powder Room at the Transcontinental, stripping off with a girl whose name he didn't even know. Not that it mattered. All he cared about was getting it on with her, and to hell with formal introductions.

It was one hell of a place, he mused as he undressed, kicking off his shoes so hard that they skidded across the white marble floor. All polished wood, Italian marble and pot-pourri. Mirrors, too, every-fucking-where. No matter where you looked, you could see yourself having sex in a dozen different positions. He wondered fleetingly if this kind of thing went on all the time in ladies' toilets, and whether he could make the grade as a transvestite . . .

She pulled her vest off over her head, and her big, soft breasts bounced into his face. He felt an almost childlike urge to nuzzle into all that lovely, warm flesh, but she was already taking her pants off, wriggling out of the tiniest little white thong, exposing her completely shaven Mound of Venus.

'You're big,' she said. 'I like my men big.' For a moment, he thought she was going to drop to her knees and go down on him right there and then; but instead, she dragged him over to the big pink velvet sofa that filled one end of the room. 'Lie down.'

It didn't cross his mind for one moment to say no. He stretched himself out on the sleek, silky pile and she planted a kiss on his upturned dick. *Oh please fuck me,* he begged silently. *Please fuck me before I explode.*

She lowered herself onto him, but not in the way he'd expected. She was facing away from him, her head bent towards his dick, her thighs on either side of his face. It was a wonderful view; the dusky-pink ripples of her cunt, all wet and glistening, bearing down on him with sudden, desperate urgency.

It wasn't until the very last moment that he realised that something was wrong, very wrong. The girl wasn't just lowering herself onto his face, she was crushing him, sitting down hard on him with all her weight, so hard that he could hardly breathe. He tried to wriggle free, to lift her off his face, but she was much, much stronger than he could ever have imagined.

He started to panic, tried to open his mouth to tell her he was drowning, suffocating, but no sound came out. Then he heard her voice:

'Lick me out.'

He was really panicking now. Every tiny breath was agony.

'Lick me out – and do it well. Or you will die.'

He began to lick. It was almost impossible. She was pressing down on him so hard, his mouth would scarcely open. His head was spinning, his lungs were aching, his whole body felt as though it was about to explode. But above all the agony was a worse pain, the terrible need to taste her flesh, and the juices of her pleasure.

As she came, her sweet wetness flooded his mouth and he felt her muscles twitch about his tongue-tip. Then she got off him. She was not smiling any more.

'Forget me. And forget all about Sylvie Montana,' she waned. 'Or next time it will not be a little innocent fun, Mr Usher, you will pay with your life.'

Now that he knew the full power of the golden box, Christian's intentions were perfectly clear. He would use that power against the Master.

The only problem was finding a way of doing so without arousing his suspicions. So finely-honed were the Master's psychic abilities that he could sense a four-leafed clover at twenty paces, never mind this magical atom bomb. Christian would have to tread very, very carefully indeed.

As luck would have it, the perfect opportunity presented itself much sooner than he could have envisaged; and only a week later, Christian found himself sitting in the audience at the Oxford Union, watching Anthony LeMaitre speaking for the motion: 'This House believes that a good government is an ethical government'.

He did not bother listening to the Master's words; he was a seasoned performer and an accomplished liar. What mattered was the audience's reaction. Christian breathed in the warm June air. Ah, the wonderful aroma of lust. You could feel it in the air, almost taste it radiating out of all those beautiful, succulent young bodies. Young lust was so potent, so utterly seductive. He could feel it strengthening him by its presence alone, and knew that tonight he could not fail.

Within ten minutes, the Master had them eating out of his hand. Some of the students were even touching their own bodies, making love to themselves as they gazed up at him in rapt attention. Surely the polls must be wrong, though Christian. These weak-minded children would slit their own throats if he asked them to.

He could wait no longer. As the Master paused to take a breath, Christian stood up in the audience, opened the lid of the box and took out the tiny spy-glass.

Instantly the Master took a step back, recoiling as if an insect had stung him. But he did not look at the box. He turned his gaze towards a blonde, athletic-looking girl directly in front of him, her lips moist and open, her generous breasts cupped in her hands like an offering, her thumbs moving rhythmically across the nipples.

Christian turned back to the box and watched the mists clearing.

What he saw there filled him with horror.

12

'Thank God I'm out of the spotlight,' sighed Andreas, burying his face in his arms.

'You're glad the Master's got a new favourite, then?' Mara smoothed warm, patchouli-scented oil into his shoulders, easing out the knots of tension. 'You're not jealous of Christian?'

Andreas let out a hollow laugh. 'Jealous? Oh very funny, ha, ha. You know damn well I'm ecstatic. Now El Presidente can't get enough of Christian, and I've been demoted to running the media campaign, he hardly notices I'm there most of the time.'

'Which suits you down to the ground?'

'Too right it does. As long as I don't balls up the party politicals, it should give us a bit more breathing space.'

'So you can relax, then.'

Andreas hesitated. 'No,' he replied, aware that he was still feeling distinctly uneasy, despite Mara's skilful hands. 'Not yet. Not by a long chalk.'

'Poor darling,' commiserated Mara, rolling him over onto his back. Her warm, slippery hand slithered down his belly and traced ever-decreasing circles round the dancing cobra of his cock. At last her fingers closed round it and he surrendered to her with little growls of pleasure. 'Just as well I can think of something to relax you, isn't it?'

Greg jabbed Cindy's number into his mobile phone and tapped his foot impatiently. 'Come on, come on.'

Something clicked dully at the other end. 'Yeah?'

'Cindy, it's Greg.'

Cindy's voice sounded less than warm and welcoming. 'It's ten past fucking two – it's the middle of the night, you tosser!'

'Yeah, I know, I'm sorry, OK? But something big's come up; I need to talk to you.'

'And it can't wait till morning?'

'It can't wait five minutes. Do you want the story of the decade, or not?'

'Oh all right – my house, half an hour, you can bring the whisky. And you'd better not disappoint

me, Greg; I can be a real bitch when I miss out on
my beauty sleep.'

Cindy looked great, even at three o'clock in the
morning with last night's lipstick smudged across
her lips. Greg tried to concentrate on the facts of
the case, but his attention kept straying to the way
the white shirt she was wearing kept falling open,
making it obvious there was nothing underneath.

She tossed her head and lolled back on the settee,
flaunting the soft brown triangle at the apex of her
thighs. 'Stop staring at my pussy, Greg, and get on
with the story.' Her tongue slid over her lips, moist
and pink as the flesh of her sex. Greg felt himself
harden uncomfortably against the crotch of his
pants. 'Tell me again about the prison.'

'We went there to try and see Alex, the guy with
the box.'

'Not about him. About her, Sylvie.' Greg saw
Cindy undo the last button on her silk shirt and
watched it fall open and slither down over her bare
arms. 'Tell me what she did.'

'She took off all her clothes and danced naked in
front of the security cameras.'

'No, what she did inside the prison. What
happened to her when she got inside.'

Greg heard Cindy's breathing growing shallow, rapid, slightly hoarse. He knew that sound. She was getting really excited; so that was why she was getting him to go over things twice, just so she could get off on the horny bits.

'Four guards took her into the showers.'

'And?' she coaxed, sliding a finger down her belly and into the soft frizz that covered her plump sex-lips.

'They tied her up and beat her. Then they had her on the floor, all four of them at once.'

Cindy purred. Her hands reached out to him and started undoing the buckle of his belt. Normally he wouldn't have protested one bit, but this wasn't what he'd planned. He'd come here to tell her what was going on, get some advice from her on what to do about Sylvie's disappearance, instead of which Cindy was more interested in seducing him on the settee.

'Cindy . . .' he began, but she had looped the belt around his neck and was using it to draw him down on top of her.

'I want you to do it to me, Greg.'

'Do . . . ?'

'Don't look at me like that.' She slipped the belt into his hand, curling his fingers over the white leather. 'Go on, beat me with it. Beat me and fuck me. Make me do all those things they made your little French girl do. You wanted to do them to her too, didn't you?'

He didn't answer, partly because he was ashamed to admit that she was right; and partly because she was now on her knees, hands on the seat of the sofa, legs apart, backside upturned like a sacrificial offering. Under the circumstances what could he do? She was his boss, she was almost as scary as Sylvie Montana, and right now she was making him so hot he just couldn't control himself any longer.

He tried an experimental swing of the belt. It made her squirm as it flicked across her buttocks, and for a moment he thought he had overdone it.

'Harder,' she ordered him. 'You're not doing it hard enough. Do it to me like they did it to Sylvie.'

He tried again. This time the smooth, white curve of flesh reddened in a thin stripe that ran diagonally across Cindy's right buttock. She gasped, arching her back, and he saw droplets of clear fluid appear at the tops of her thighs, dripping out of her like nectar squeezed from a flower-bud.

'Yes . . . yes . . . but harder, *harder*! And keep on talking, keep on telling me what they did to her . . .'

Cindy twisted and turned as the belt came

slashing down, again and again, raising a criss-cross pattern of red welts. They must have caused her pain, but the only sounds she made were moans and groans of pleasure. Her backside pushed itself towards him, her arse-cheeks opening, offering him the tight amber blossom of her anus.

'Fuck me,' she ordered him. 'Fuck me in the arse.'

Greased with the juices from her pussy, he slid into her tight sheath like a well-oiled sword into its scabbard. He felt her muscles clench about him with every thrust, with every stroke of the belt on her hungry flesh and was sure he could not last beyond a few seconds. But somehow she took him to the edge and held him there, forcing him to the very limits of self-control then refusing to let him cross the line. It was pure torture. And it was fantastic.

By the time she took pity on him and squeezed the juice out of his swollen balls, he was fucking on auto-pilot, too far gone to even try and regain the upper hand.

Satisfied at last, she pushed him away. Totally spent, he rolled sideways and found himself gazing up into her laughing face.

'Well,' she commented, kissing a fingertip and

pressing it to his lips, 'that was quite some fairy-story.'

He got to his knees and seized her by the wrists. 'Weren't you listening to me, Cindy? It's true, all of it. Every word.'

'Oh, yeah, sure it is.' Freeing her hand, she slid it over his face and began to stroke his hair. 'Magic boxes that make you fuck. You've got a great imagination, Greg, I'll give you that.'

'What do I have to do to make you believe me?'

'There's nothing you can do.' She was nuzzling his neck now. 'Nothing at all.'

He felt something scratch his throat and he drew back, suddenly alarmed. Cindy was smiling at him, sexy mouth open, lips full and moist.

'Nobody'd ever believe that story, Greg.' Her sharp little teeth glittered in the lamplight. 'Even if they ever got a chance to hear it.'

He didn't hear what she said next. Two seconds later he passed out on the Axminster.

'No, no, no, no, noooo,' moaned the she-twin, tears spilling down her face as she watched her finger grow back for the hundredth time. The knife shook in her hand, her blood vanishing into thin air almost as soon as it soiled the blade.

'It is no use.' Her brother lashed out at a masked male slave, making him stagger sideways, his cock grossly stretched and distended by the iron weights which hung from it on a cruelly taught chain. 'He has made us different; he has broken the symmetry; we can never be one again.'

The slave cowered in the corner, the iron weights swinging, his flesh studded with the four-inch nails his master had driven into him as punishment for yet another imagined crime. His master had been acting with unaccustomed savagery ever since his finger had been taken from him; none of the slaves had escaped his wrath.

Christian smiled as he walked into the apartment. All in all, things had worked out rather well so far. When he had found the twins, they had been distraught, discordant, the she-twin endlessly cutting off her finger and watching it regrow. Frankly, they had been positively suicidal: not that suicide would serve any purpose for them, since they were doomed to immortality.

And doomed was the word. Once-identical Docklands lofts had begun to go in separate directions. Identical Persian cats had taken to tearing lumps out of each other. Identical pleasures had diverged, becoming conflicting perversions. Little by little, the twins were peeling apart like the two halves of some rotting fruit.

They were perfect prey for Christian.

He walked across to the she-twin, who was sitting weeping at the table, surrounded by dozens of sharp knives. As she prepared to cut herself again, he placed a hand on hers.

'I can restore your balance.'

She looked up at him with wondering eyes; suspicious, hardly daring to hope.

'How can this be?' demanded her brother.

Christian amused himself with a dramatic pause. He loved drama, revelled in the feeling of power it gave him over other creatures. After a few delicious seconds, he placed the attache case on the table and clicked it open. The box lay inside, small and beautiful and malevolent on a bed of crimson velvet.

'The box!' cried the she-twin, lunging for it. 'He has the box!'

But Christian slammed the case shut and consigned it to invisibility with a sharp click of his fingers. One could not be too careful with the key to ultimate power.

'Yes children, I have it. Think of its power, think of what it could do for you. For *us*. In time, even revenge could be yours.'

The twins huddled together, clinging to each other, eyes wide with need.

'Give it to us, give it to us!'

He shook his head. 'First, you must prove that you deserve it. First, you must satisfy my pleasure.'

When Greg woke up, the first thing he did was feel his own neck. Thank God for that, not a scratch. It must have been a horrible dream.

Unfortunately it wasn't a dream, as he realised when he opened his eyes and looked around him. He wasn't in his own bed, or Sylvie's, or on Cindy's settee for that matter. He was in a vast attic room, all done out on pale wood like an Ikea catalogue, but there the resemblance ended. He'd never actually been to Scandinavia, but he had a hunch that even the average broad-minded Swede drew the line at having a medieval torture-rack in the middle of his front room.

Racks, punishment tables, wall bars jangling with straps and chains and things he couldn't even guess at. Cages, hanging from the ceiling. A collection of whips, neatly arranged on the wall. An iron maiden straight out of Dracula's castle. A smell of blood and sex . . .

'Good morning, Mr Usher. Did you sleep well?'

His entire being lurched as he turned round groggily, and saw the welcoming committee. The man was in the middle – the young, arrogant one he'd seen coming out of Lea Hall prison in a limo. The Master's new campaign manager. And on either side . . .

'Oh. My God. Is that really you?'

He didn't need to ask. In all honesty, you couldn't mistake Sylvie and Cindy for anybody else, but he'd never seen them like this before, corseted in boned black leather, with their breasts and buttocks bare, and thigh-high boots with heels like an assassin's knife. Collars of matching black crystal glittered at their throats, not quite masking the tiny, fresh scars of their initiation.

'Greg,' smiled Cindy, her eyes filled with malevolent lust.

'Greg, *chéri*. We have waited for you so long . . .'

Oh, shit, thought Greg as he looked into those predatory eyes. He pinched himself. All that did was make him wince. This was not a dream; he had been invited here to breakfast and, unless he was very much mistaken, he was about to be the main course.

'What the bloody hell is going on?' he demanded,

trying to sound more aggressive than he felt.

Christian casually drew a knife-blade across his own arm and watched indulgently as Sylvie and Cindy fought to lap up the droplets of blood before the wound closed up and disappeared.

'You are perhaps wondering why you are still alive, Mr Usher,' he remarked.

'Actually, I'm quite happy being alive; that's fine by me. Dead is what I'm not so keen on.'

'Quite. Well you may like to know that I have kept you alive for a reason. You are intelligent, analytical, open-minded . . .'

'Thanks,' said Greg. It was the best reference he'd ever had. 'Can I have that in writing?'

'. . . over-sexed – and most importantly, human. I have uses for an undetectable spy, Mr Usher. An undetectable *human* spy.'

Greg swallowed. 'A *spy*?'

'Compliance will be handsomely rewarded. Oh – and, by the way, the alternative is death.' Christian yawned, and signalled to the vamps. 'Sylvie, Lucinda, you may feed now. But do not bite him or you will feel the sting of my wrath. I have plans for Mr Usher.'

He watched in mild amusement as they went to work with their agile tongues. The human was a ridiculously easy conquest for the sluts, as much a slave of his base desires as they were of theirs. He would serve him well.

He thought back to the Oxford Union, and the vision the box had given him of the Master's secret desire. The desire to be crushed totally, to be at last humiliated by a superior opponent, destroyed utterly and consigned to eternal oblivion.

It was a fine, seductive fantasy. And Christian was caught up in it now, a prisoner of the box; unable to escape from the compulsion to carry it out. He knew that he must destroy the Master, and that he must to do completely; for the slightest ounce of failure, and the Master would eat his soul.

Epilogue

Andreas reached into his pocket, took out the tape and slid it along the bar.

'There you go, Greg; you'd better have this. You might find some of it useful.'

Greg contemplated it with grim humour. 'We always used to say it was you and me against the world. And now it bloody well is.'

Andreas glanced round. 'Just take it, will you? Somebody might see.'

He picked it up and dropped it into his inside pocket. 'How do I know I can trust you? You're a flaming vampire.'

'No, I'm not, I told you. I'm just trapped in a vampire's body, don't you ever listen?'

'All right, you're *partly* a vampire.'

'And you're a vampire's secret agent,' Andreas reminded him, draining his beer-glass. 'So how can *I* trust *you*?'

'Fair point,' conceded Greg. He nodded towards the empty glass. 'Time for another?'

'Go on, then.' Andreas's attention wandered as Greg got the drinks in. 'Blimey.' He nudged Greg in the ribs.

'Ow. What's that for?'

Andreas gestured towards five feet-six of blonde gorgeousness, ordering a cocktail at the far end of the bar. 'Will you look at the arse on that.'

They gazed besottedly at the girl, independently weighing up their chances. 'Hey,' said Greg, grinning cheesily. 'She's smiling at me.'

'You mean she's smiling at *me*.' Andreas returned the smile with a debonair wave. 'Well, well, look – she's got a friend.'

The glamorous redhead in the low-cut top turned heads right across the hotel bar as she walked over to join the blonde.

'Right.' Greg picked up his drink. 'Are you up for it then?'

'What about Cindy?'

'What about Mara?'

They exchanged a theatrical wink.

'Us against the world eh?'

Andreas chuckled. 'As long as our girlfriends don't find out.'

More Erotic Fiction from Headline Delta

Bonjour Amour

EROTIC DREAMS OF PARIS IN THE 1950s

Marie-Claire Villefranche

Odette Charron is twenty-three years old with enchanting green eyes, few inhibitions and a determination to make it as a big-time fashion model. At present she is distinctly small-time. So a meeting with important fashion-illustrator Laurent Breville represents an opportunity not to be missed.

Unfortunately, Laurent has a fiancée to whom he is tediously faithful. But Odette has the kind of face and figure which can chase such mundane commitments from his mind. For her, Laurent is the first step on the ladder of success and she intends to walk all over him. What's more, he's going to love it . . .

FICTION / EROTICA 0 7472 4803 6